The Other Side of the Line

By

James F. Ford, Jr., Ph.D.

Life is good!

Jim

SHIRES PRESS

4869 Main Street
P.O. Box 2200
Manchester Center, VT 05255
www.northshire.com

The Other Side of the Line

ISBN: 978-1-60571-410-3

Building Community, One Book at a Time
*A family-owned, independent bookstore in
Manchester Ctr., VT, since 1976 and Saratoga Springs, NY since 2013.
We are committed to excellence in bookselling.
The Northshire Bookstore's mission is to serve as a resource for
information, ideas, and entertainment while honoring the needs
of customers, staff, and community.*

Printed in the United States of America

Dedication

Law Enforcement is a noble profession. To the men and women who put their lives on the line every day, thank you.

Preface

As a child of the fifties, I attended Saint Joseph's School in Maplewood, NJ and grew up Roman Catholic. Though not to a fanatical degree, my faith and spirituality were important to me and still are to this day. When I was ten years old, our family moved from the Vauxhall section of Union to the Battle Hill Section of Union. I transferred to Battle Hill School in the sixth grade. All through junior high and high school, I thought about only three careers: priesthood, education, and law enforcement. While a junior in high school and working part-time at the A&P in Union on Morris Avenue and Spruce Street, I met Debbie, and we soon began dating. After graduating high school, I attended Union County College for two years and then transferred to Glassboro State College (now Rowan University). Debbie went to the University of New Hampshire for two years and then transferred to Seton Hall University. We married right after graduation. Then I needed a job!

The common denominator between all three of the professions in which I was interested was that they all involved helping others. In high school, I was part of the

Union Junior Police Department. This organization operated within the Union Police Department, though we did not have arrest powers or the ability to carry a firearm. As teens, we were mostly utilized at parades, dances, shows and church traffic. One "Mischief Night" was a particular turning point for me. I was in the Union Police Department when police officers arrested an individual for shoplifting and assault. I felt a rush of adrenaline and was convinced that this was the career I wanted to enter.

While in college, I still entertained the idea of priesthood. However, I was leaning more toward a career in law enforcement; I was also falling in love with Debbie and the consequent expectations of marriage. I knew that you could not be a priest and a spouse at the same time. There are more similarities between priesthood and law enforcement than you might imagine. As I describe later in the book, I was hired as a police officer, and during my tenth year in this profession, I returned to college for my master's degree. I attended and graduated from Seton Hall University with a master's degree in education. A year prior to retiring from the police department, I was given the opportunity to be an adjunct professor at the College of Saint Elizabeth in Morristown, NJ. I soon developed a love of teaching and sharing my knowledge and experience with students. I then discovered that I would need a doctoral degree to teach full-time at a four-year college. After conducting an exhaustive search for a very good school, I discovered Capella University and enrolled. Four and a half years later, I graduated with my Ph.D.

After I returned home from Capella University's commencement ceremony in San Francisco, I had a doctor's appointment. My doctor is Burton Tucker, and for years his practice was on Shunpike Road at the corner of Noe Avenue in Chatham Township. The checkup went well, and I believe I was his last patient of the day. Burt could not have been happier for me, but he then suggested that I should really write a book. "A book?" I said. "Yeah, sure." He was serious, though, and I still remember him saying, "Your book would be different. We [the public] always read about the big city cops who make drug busts or organized crime or gang stories, but no one really writes about the type of work and sacrifices that police officers such as yourself made. I know the sacrifices you made by treating you all these years and knowing your family." So here I am with my book, finally. At each doctor's appointment between then and now, Burt has always asked how the book is coming along. Finally and recently he said to me, "I want to read the book before I die." I told him my stalling was keeping him alive.

Acknowledgements

It is with much gratitude that I thank the following individuals:

Burton Tucker, M.D for suggesting I write the book and his relentless devotion to its completion. George Sirgiovanni, Ph.D for his friendship, professional editing and advice. Brian J. Ford, M.A. for presenting me with the "Thin Blue Line Flag", which is featured on the back cover.

Lastly, to the men and women of the Chatham Township Police Department.

How many times have we heard in our life, I could write a book…well, I did!

History 101

It is widely believed that Morris County was carved out of Hunterdon County in 1738 due to increasing population in Hunterdon. In 1740 the Morris County courts convened and divided the county into three townships: Morris, Hanover, and Pequannock. In 1806 Chatham Township incorporated and included the areas that are now known as Chatham Borough, Madison, and Florham Park. The name Chatham was derived from Sir William Pitt, the elder of Chatham, who had spoken in favor of the colonists in Parliament. Many of you may have heard of Chatham but may not have realized there are two Chathams in Morris County. Chatham Borough is a little over two square miles and Chatham Township a little over nine square miles. These areas were connected by toll roads and turnpikes primarily built by private corporations to transport their goods to market. Local residents later built Shunpike Road to avoid paying tolls. The most important development in transportation was probably the arrival of Morris and Essex Railroad in 1837. The subsequent population increase eventually resulted in Chatham, Madison, and Florham Park incorporating as separate boroughs.

Chatham also became a center of the rose growing industry in the 1870s and 1880s. Louis M. Noe's greenhouses were known for the American Beauty rose, which had a stem five feet long. The years between the Civil War and World War I were a period of quiet living and simple pleasures. Chatham's reputation as a fine, healthy place to live grew and brought a tourist trade. There was a five-year ban on construction during World War II, but soon after the ban was lifted, families began building luxurious homes that replaced many large farms. Former rose farms became two major shopping centers at the corner of Hickory Tree, named for a hickory tree planted during President Madison's term.

In the early 1960s, Chatham Township had quite a fight on its hands. The New York and New Jersey Port Authority was making plans to build a third major airport in the region. This "jetport" was going to be where the Great Swamp is located today. The plans were leaked to the New York Times, and the news caused a stir in the community. A successful campaign was initiated, and eventually the plan for the "jetport" was defeated a few years later. Among the reasons cited were flood control, wildlife, aesthetics, and the area's ecological value. The Great Swamp's treasures caused the U.S. Fish and Wildlife Service to establish it as a Wildlife Refuge, the first National Wilderness Area east of the Mississippi River.

Today Chatham Township has many fine homes, townhouses, garden apartments, and condominiums and is very attractive to suburbanites with its convenient rail, bus, and highway connections to New York and three major airports. There are many cultural opportunities including historical sites, art museums, gardens, and concert venues. The College of Saint Elizabeth, Drew University, and Fairleigh Dickinson are Chatham's higher education neighbors that offer a variety of programs.

How It All Began

Police jobs in the late seventies and early eighties were few and far between. Taking a civil service test for the position of police officer usually meant competing against hundreds of other applicants at the time of the test and thousands of applicants statewide. You could also apply to be a police officer in municipalities that were not civil service; this usually meant that a "chief's test" was administered by the town. Civil service rules allowed disabled veterans and veterans to go to the top of the list over non-veterans. The only hope that non-veterans had was that civil service would reach them wherever they fell on the list. Then you had to deal with the "rule of three." The "rule of three" enabled civil service communities to choose one of three top candidates. If a municipality was hiring four officers, it could either hire the highest ranked four or use the "rule of three." Could municipalities skip the first two candidates to get to the third? Yes! This practice meant, in effect, that someone ranked twelfth could be hired.

Realizing that it was going to be very difficult to be hired through civil service, I paid a fee to a resume service and learned how to construct a resume. I decided to apply to fifty municipalities and sent a resume to each. I was working the steady midnight shift at Seton Hall University as a campus patrol officer. My wife of only a few months was an elementary school teacher at Sacred Heart Catholic School in Elizabeth, NJ. So she worked days and I worked nights; we saw each other when she came home from work, and then I went to work at 11 p.m. When I came home from work, she left for work. My days off were Tuesdays and Wednesdays—not many family gatherings happened on those days. My wife's days off were the weekends. Trying to make social engagements with family and friends was close to impossible.

Figuring it would add to my resume, I continued to work at the university as a campus police officer. I mailed out fifty resumes in hopes of hearing from someone regarding a police officer position. In late January 1976, I received a phone call from the captain of the Chatham Township Police Department, who indicated that they were interested in me and asked whether I was available for an interview. I said yes, I most certainly would be available. I could not wait for my wife to come home from school so I could tell her. In the meantime, I told my father because I did not know where this town was. I had heard of Chatham Township and Chatham Borough but was not sure where they were located.

On the day of the interview, my father drove me since he knew of the town. I was dressed in a suit and tie and was naturally nervous. I remember the day was cold and the sky was clear with a bright blue sky. The appointment was scheduled for 11 a.m. I was early and rode around the town to see its boundaries. The police department was located in an old house near a public park (Nash Field) and a beautifully manicured golf course, which later would go on to host the LPGA tournament. I walked into the police department and was greeted by the desk sergeant, who was seated right in front of the door. To the right of the entrance was the secretary's desk. There was a narrow hallway that led to the chief and captain's office. Opposite their office was a desk that officers used to prepare their reports. There was another office that contained three desks, one for the detective lieutenant and the other two for detectives. I learned that one of the detectives handled juvenile cases, and the other detective handled the rest. I was interviewed by the chief of police, captain, detective lieutenant, patrol lieutenant, and desk sergeant in the room that was shared by the captain and chief of police. The room was no larger than eight by ten feet, held two desks and filing cabinets, and had a door that exited to the outside. I did not know that I was going to be interviewed by five officers. After answering the usual questions about why I wanted to be a police officer, why there, and how I prepared myself for the position, all the officers asked a question or two. The interview lasted about an hour. I left feeling confident, but you can never be certain about an interview. After all, I didn't know how many more candidates were being interviewed. I remember coming home and feeling very good about the interview, but I knew I had to go to work that night. When my wife came home, I told her how it went and was hopeful. My wife had known since we started dating that I wanted to be a police officer. My grandfather on my father's side had been a police officer in the neighboring community of Summit for a number of years. I never knew my grandfather because he died when my father was in his teens. But everyone I met always told me that Dennis (Denny) Ford was a fine officer, respected and as honest as the day is long.

Weeks passed after my interview at Chatham Township, and I did not hear anything. In the meantime, I realized that the steady night shift was not the best shift to be working, especially as I was newly married. I knew I had to make a career change and started looking for a new job again. I was not eating or sleeping right and wanted as close to a job with normal hours as I could find. A few weeks later in the beginning of March, I received a call from the captain of the Chatham Township Police Department. He informed me that the township committee now wanted to interview all the candidates and that I was still in the running. During our conversation, the captain asked, "You did graduate from college, right?" I said "Yes, I graduated from Glassboro State College in May 1975 with my bachelor's degree in law and justice." I knew I had made a copy of my diploma and submitted it with the resume, but the captain could not find it.

The date for the oral interview with the township committee was scheduled for the middle of March at 7:30 p.m. It was snowing with the wind blowing—winter's last call. I remember standing on the first floor of this old two-story schoolhouse that had been converted into the offices for the town hall. I met the other candidates, and though we exchanged pleasantries and wished each other well, we were not kidding anyone. I remember one of them was a veteran and two of them were flashy dressers. I was dressed in a nice suit and felt very confident. All seven of us were going for one position. I wanted the job more! I was escorted to the second floor where the town hall offices were and met all the township committee members. The chief of police was there along with the town clerk. One of the questions I was asked in the interview was why I wanted to be a police officer and what I hoped to do if I got the position. I told them the truth: I was genuinely interested in helping people, and it was not all about arresting people or writing summonses. I also felt that working in the town would allow me to do my job, to do it well, and to not be rushed like in other busier communities. If I got the job, I was hoping to be chief of police someday.

Just two days prior to this interview, I had responded to an ad for a security management position with Bamberger's Department store. After a quick interview I got hired as an assistant manager in training for that store's security department. I think what helped me secure that position was my bachelor's degree and the manager training I received while working for the A&P food stores and attending Union County College. The training took place at their store headquarters in Newark, NJ. I figured being trained there was rather the proving ground. If you could work there, you could work in any of their department stores. While there I met another young man, and it appeared that the two of us would train together and later be assigned to our stores. I was excited about the new position; I knew my wife was excited for me but also worried about my working in Newark.

The next day, my second day at Bamberger's, the other young man and I had lunch together, and I asked him what he had done before coming to Bamberger's. He told me that he had been hired as a police officer in the same town in which I had interviewed the previous night, but after discussing it with his fiancée, he had decided to turn it down. I found his decision interesting but did not say anything. The next morning I received a call from the Chatham captain, and he asked me if I was still interested in the police officer position. I said, "Sure, I am." He told me that the township committee had decided on me, but I had to get a physical and psychological checkup and be outfitted in uniforms within three days. The police department was scheduling all of these activities. I called Bamberger's and gave them my notice, but I told them I couldn't give the usual two weeks because of the short notice and timing of the job offer. The director of security was disappointed but understood and wished me well. A dream of mine came true on March 15, 1976; it was the day I was sworn in as a police officer, and my life forever changed.

The Police Academy

Police departments have the choice between sending their new officers to Sea Girt, which is where the New Jersey State Police trains municipal officers, or sending newly hired officers to a county police academy, provided they have an opening. Our town chose to send their officers to the Morris County Police Academy. It was a well-run and highly disciplined academy. The classes were taught mostly by active full-time officers who specialized in a particular area and who, along with teaching academics to the recruits, shared their experiences with the class. It was not all "war stories." Some of the best and brightest officers served as instructors.

On the first day we met the Morris County Police Academy Director Howard Runyon, who was also the chief of police in Passaic Township (now Long Hill Township). The first day was part orientation and part actual class work. Our class schedule was explained to us thoroughly, as were the consequences for missing classes or assignments. The first day was interesting for many of us who didn't know each other, and it provided us with an opportunity to meet others and to share our hopes and expectations. Our class was made up of mostly municipal police officers and a few county park officers; the rest consisted of officers from the Morris County Sheriff's Department. Upon graduation we would all be certified police officers in the state of New Jersey. The days started for us at 6:45 a.m., and physical fitness was always the first class of the day. We were timed for showers, getting dressed, and readying ourselves for inspections, which were conducted by either the academy director or visiting chiefs of police. Everything from your hat to your shoes had to be inspected. Some of the inspections were run by officers who thought they were drill sergeants from the U.S. Marines. After the inspection there was a brief break, which was followed by academics. The academics curriculum consisted of classes on search and seizure, drug law, motor vehicle, report writing, criminal investigation, crime scene processing, interviewing techniques, and other police-related topics. These classes lasted most of the day and ended between 4:00 and 5:00 p.m. We were allowed a half-hour for lunch and socializing.

Our class was scheduled for sixteen weeks. Each class usually loses a few of the recruits for various reasons. These reasons can include an inability to take the physical training, the structure of the day, and the academics. Some came into the academy with the attitude that they were God's gift to the world, and they soon found out that they were nothing while in training. Some of the officers' egos could not handle it, and they soon found themselves out of the academy. Sending an officer to the police academy is an investment from the community. If an officer is hired after the first of the year and enters a police academy in March, he or she will graduate sometime in June and return to his or her respective police department. Most New Jersey municipalities' budgets are prepared in the fall and approved in early spring, which is when officers are most likely to be hired. Police academies normally run two classes a year: one class in the winter and one class in the fall. The point is that if a recruit washes out or gets dismissed from the academy, the town then has to wait until the next class to enroll a new recruit. In theory, an officer can be hired to replace the one who resigned or was dismissed, but in actuality it takes a good year for an officer to be fully trained and operational.

In my case, I had to learn the streets of my town in a hurry because the squad on which I was going to work had officers going on vacation. On weekends I rode with officers from the police department to try to learn the streets. One of the officers was going away for the month of July, and the other was going away for the month of August. Yes, you guessed it: no one really cared about my time, as I was the junior officer. But that was okay with me.

Probably the most grueling part of our training was physical fitness. The physical fitness training consisted mostly of sit-ups, push-ups, squat thrusts, a one-and-a-half mile run, pull-ups, and scaling a six-foot wall. I thought the toughest part was the one-and-a-half mile run. Most of us worked out on weekends even though we should have given our muscles time to relax. Our physical fitness instructor was a lieutenant from the Morris Township Police Department. He was committed to training the recruits to be in the best physical shape they could possibly be in. It's ironic how we all used to dread taking PT every morning, but I believe he was the most respected instructor we had over the course of the training. There were the usual physical injuries that accompany physical training; even the most physically fit officer can suffer some type of injury. Teamwork was one of the most important aspects of the physical training. Our class was fortunate to have members who encouraged others, especially officers who were struggling. Officers who do not meet the academic standards or the physical fitness qualifications are usually dismissed in the first few weeks. It should be noted that many of the officers—not all—had received a few months' notice before attending the academy and thus were able to prepare for the physical fitness routines. Our class had a few older officers; while most of us were in our twenties, there were also some in their late thirties and early forties. They were in incredible shape for their age. Though some of the older recruits still struggled all sixteen weeks, everyone passed the physical fitness portion of the training.

Firearms training was a particularly interesting block of instruction. Some of us were used to handling firearms while others were not. We had a few officers who did not have any prior training and still did better than some of the recruits who had had prior exposure to firearms. Several certified firearms instructors were assigned to two or three recruits. Besides handgun qualification, we had to become proficient in the use of shotguns. Several hundred rounds of ammunition were spent in qualifying. For those of you not used to firing a shotgun, it's an experience one does not soon forget. There are certain phrases that stick with you throughout your career. I still remember one of them: "Slowly squeeze the trigger and be surprised when the gun goes off."

Getting exposed to tear gas was one of the most memorable aspects of the training we went through at the police academy. We had to experience what it was like to feel the effects of tear gas by being exposed to it ourselves. We were huddled in one of the fire towers, and we had on tear gas masks so we would know what that was like. Then the fun part came: we had to take them off while the tear gas was still present. Needless to say, the recruits who had asthma or other respiratory illnesses were not amused—nor were they excused from the training session. Afterward, we poured gallons of water on our faces and eyes. Some recruits threatened lawsuits or other legal action for exposing us to the tear gas, but the next day, those ideas were vacated. Most of the recruits had been upset in the moment. We joked when it was over, and someone said, "Let's hope we don't have to be shot to see if our bullet proof vests work!" Almost every instructor drilled into us the idea that it was better to be judged by six than carried by six. Basically, it is better to have a jury of six judge you than have six people carry you to your grave.

We had several academic tests every week, and the various subjects included criminal law, motor vehicle laws, juvenile laws, search and seizure, and drug laws. Our scores were posted according to our social security numbers. If a recruit was having a problem in any area, it wasn't long before his or her police department contacted him or her and asked what the problem was and whether there was anything they could do to help. Most police academies sponsored in-service and mandatory training for police officers. I knew when I started that my chief and the police academy director were not only colleagues but also good friends. Oh yeah, bring on the pressure!

At the end of the training, several awards were given out. Awards included those for highest academic achievement, highest academic scores, most improved, and top firearms scorer. After a few weeks, the recruits were quite competitive with each other. We were caught up in trying to get the highest score in any of the areas. It was mandatory for all recruits to keep a notebook. The academy staff inspected the notebooks weekly. I am very proud to say that my academy notebook and that of another officer were the best in the academy while I was enrolled. I still have my six notebook binders, which measure about three to four inches thick; I did refer to them from time to time throughout my career.

I remember graduation day; it was on June 15th. It was a warm sunny day with blue skies and puffy clouds. Besides my wife, I was able to invite other guests as well. My mother, father, and paternal grandmother were invited along with my mother-in-law and father-in-law. Graduation day was on a Friday, and in attendance were the chief and other representatives from my police department. I remember the chief coming over, congratulating me, and telling me I was off for the weekend and to report Monday for day shift, which was 8 a.m. to 4 p.m. The recruits sat in the large auditorium and were called up in alphabetical order. The academy director, a representative from the New Jersey Police Training Commission, and representatives from our own departments presented us with our diplomas. After the ceremony, we retreated into the multi-purpose room to have refreshments and mingle with other recruits and their families.

After the social event in the multi-purpose room, we all departed. We promised to stay in touch and wondered who would not last on the job. To celebrate, my family and I went to the William Pitt Restaurant in Chatham for lunch. It was the last weekend I was off for a long time. The working schedule for my police department was counterclockwise, but we changed shifts every week. We worked five days on and two days off, five days on and two days off, and then five days on and one day off. The department owed us a day every cycle, which provided us with "owed days." We could take them off whenever we wanted, provided the minimum manpower was met. The minimum manpower was two patrol officers on the road and, usually, a sergeant who worked the desk. The town was geographically divided into three zones: A, B, and C. The C zone was the floater car, which still had to patrol within certain boundaries. The A car was the Green Village car, and the B car was known as the Long Hill car.

Through the years the town grew in population with Chatham Glen's development, the Dodge Estate, Giralda Farms, and other tracts of land that were building residences. Our schools merged after I was on the force for a few years, and our business district grew. The town is geographically shaped like a C around the Great Swamp, which presented its own challenges. The police department grew as large as thirty-one officers at one point. At our strongest, we had a chief, three lieutenants, five sergeants, three detectives, two to four traffic safety officers, sixteen patrolmen, and four dispatchers. After an increase in personnel, we lost a few good officers to other agencies, mostly because the opportunities were greater in agencies larger than ours. There were shifts when it seemed like we were falling over each other and couldn't wait to respond to calls. We were fortunate to have two wonderfully trained volunteer fire departments and a great first aid squad that served both the borough and the township. All these volunteers responded from their homes or from town if they were working. Generally, the police department worked very well with these agencies, and we respected each other.

The Rookie Years: 1976-1977

After graduating from the police academy in the middle of June 1976, I spent the remainder of that month working dayshift, during which I learned the streets, filled out health care and pension forms, and met many of the townspeople. When I began my career in 1976, our town had close to 7,500 residents. When I retired in 2002, we had approximately 11,000 residents. The captain had diligently worked with the township committee and various boards like zoning and planning on a new police facility. The police department had outgrown its present location, which was an old Cape Cod-style home.

When you walked in the front door of the old headquarters, there was a desk where the desk sergeant or officer in charge sat. Next to that desk was the chief's secretary's desk; the officers would eat their dinners or lunches there when she wasn't in the building. Down the hall, the room to the left was shared as an office between the chief and captain. Opposite that room was a kitchen with a pocket door that was used more as a dark room. Chatham Township Police Department used to take its own crime scene and accident scene photos and develop them. The police photographer was also responsible for taking pictures of special events in town, such as when elected officials were sworn into office or residents were being honored at the town hall. The local newspapers loved that the police took the pictures. They were black and white photos, and we used an old 5x7 Graphix camera.

The next room was the detective bureau; at that time there were two detectives and a detective lieutenant. One of the detectives was assigned to handle juveniles, while the other handled general investigations. There were times when prisoners were handcuffed to a post or ring on the porch of the police station. Back then our municipal court also conducted business in the police station. Remember, this was a Cape Cod-style home with four rooms and a second floor that was only used for storage. I guess I was fortunate to have only worked a few months in the so-called "old building"; the new building was a quarter mile away and across from the Fairmount Country Club.

I met some interesting people during my first year as a police officer. One of the most colorful characters was a woman named Martha. Martha was in her mid-thirties and then married to a gentleman named Oscar who was about twenty years older than she. One time while working the day shift, I had to work the desk, which meant greeting the public, answering the phones, and dispatching police, fire, or first squad personnel to calls for service. I hadn't been sitting on the desk for longer than ten minutes when this woman walked in covered in what looked like oil and dirt and wearing old jeans and an off-white button-down shirt. She came up to me, proceeded to give me a big hug, and said, "Welcome to the force!" Minutes later other officers came out of their offices, laughed, and said, "Well, we see that you met Martha." Minutes later her husband walked in and introduced himself. In order for companies to do door-to-door business in town or to go house-to-house, they needed a permit; otherwise, they would have been in violation of a local ordinance. Martha and her husband were in the driveway sealcoating business. I later learned that it had been planned for Martha and her husband to meet me that way.

One of the main duties the night shift had to perform before they went off duty was to be present at one of the banks when it opened for the day. We had to wait for one of the bank officials to arrive, walk him or her inside, and make sure everything was okay, even though it had been secure all night. Not many know this, but the banks back then were not alarmed for security reasons. The bank vault and panic buttons were active, but someone could break in during the night and lie in wait. I thought it was strange that out of the three banks in town, this was the only one that needed us. Maybe in another book I will speculate on the reason. After working all night, most officers just wanted to go home. I used to be annoyed whenever the bank employee arrived late. Hey, they were just starting their day, and mine was over. But if you missed going to the bank, you needed a valid reason, such as a bad accident or a crime-in-progress call. If you didn't have a valid reason, the patrol lieutenant would speak to you the next morning.

Another ritual was that you really couldn't talk police work until the patrol lieutenant had had his buttered roll and coffee. This particular person had a heart of gold and was responsible for showing me around the first few days and teaching me the ropes. I never forgot one of the most valuable lessons I learned from him. He used to say that when it comes to traffic enforcement, you don't need to be a ticketron; you had your whole career to write tickets. He also offered this advice: try and give the township residents a break if you can. I told him that I would use good discretion for all, not only township residents. Education is a big part of law enforcement, and as a police officer, you can tell whether or not someone you stopped has learned from his or her mistake. My general approach to everyone was the same: treat everyone fairly and objectively.

Another ritual was escorting people to the bank with cash receipts from the three schools in town. Every day when school was in session you had to go to the high school and two elementary schools, pick up a cafeteria worker, and drive her to the bank, which was the same bank as in the morning. You walked her inside so she could deposit the day's receipts and then returned her to the school. The brass frowned upon our stopping cars, which could have delayed the completion of the escort. You see, after the high school, you then had stop at another elementary school on the way to the bank and pick up those receipts. Taking the woman to the bank was good for public relations. A few years later the schools invested in a safe and other means of transporting monies. They were told that they could not count on the police to always be there; after all, we might have had to do real police work.

One of the strangest duties we had was to take a resident shopping for his weekly grocery order. Now, neither this individual nor the relative he lived with had a driver's license. So a call would come over the radio to pick up Asa and bring him to the A&P in the Chatham Mall; later, we would go back for him and transport him home. Yes, we helped him get his bags into the car and the house. This practice was allowed because the resident was elderly and did not have any means of transportation. This occurred for a few years until someone in his family took him in and they sold the house and property. The Chatham Squash Club sits on the site today. It was not uncommon for lifelong residents to stop by the police station for a cup of coffee or just to chat with whoever was on duty.

One of my unique duties was to respond to the Fairmount Country Club's Golf Course. When they had a shotgun start, the only way all the golfers knew when to begin was with the use of the police siren. So we would respond to the pool area, let the siren wail for a good minute, and then travel back to the clubhouse where hopefully everyone had started the game on time.

One of our many tasks on the night shift was to physically check all of our schools, which meant walking around and checking doors and windows. Besides schools, malls, professional buildings, and houses of worship were also checked. But the schools were the main concern. If we found a door or window open, usually a custodian was called out—and it didn't matter the time of night. Back then we were working eight hour shifts, and the schools were usually checked closer to the beginning of the shift. Of course, no one enjoyed making the call to wake someone up, and you can bet that the person who had to come out didn't appreciate it.

There were several times when the doors were found ajar and windows left open, and during our check of the building, local teenagers were found in the high school's chemistry labs. One night in particular a resident from a neighboring street reported seeing a light flashing in the high school. Several of us officers approached the school in radio silence—since many people had police scanners— and as a result several teenagers were apprehended. Another favorite trick of the kids was to climb onto the roof of the schools and, as soon as the police were summoned, to exit the roof and flee into the woods.

Before I was on my own in a patrol vehicle, I was assigned to a training officer. The training officer was a well–rounded, seasoned officer. He also conducted the bicycle safety and stranger danger talks in the school. When you're riding with a partner, you get to know the person pretty well. Richard was his first name, and he was very thorough in his training. Dick (Richard) was my FTO (field training officer) and basically taught me how to handle calls. In the academy you are taught basic procedures and state laws, but after going to your own town, you have to learn its ordinances and regulations. When Debbie and I were expecting our first child, Dick and his wife Patty had a baby shower for her at their home. When the department was small in size, we were all like family. A few years later our department had promotional testing, and Richard became a patrol sergeant. Eventually, he was promoted to detective lieutenant and retired as a captain. I worked with him in all of his ranks until he retired.

Which Way Did the Horse Go?

One of the first calls I received while on patrol was very memorable. "Headquarters to 30," I heard in my patrol car. "30," I answered. "Report of a horse running down Green Village Road by the post office heading toward Green Village Center." My first thought was, "What the hell! What do I know about catching a horse?" I tried to remember which week of police academy training covered this topic. Well, they hadn't gone over it; though they tried, they couldn't cover every type of incident. It was important to prevent the horse from being struck or striking a vehicle. One of the Green Village firemen happened to be outside and mentioned to me that he thought the horse looked familiar. If he was right, its owner lived off Green Village Road. Sure enough, all I needed to do was follow the horse, and he ran back home. The owner was glad to see his horse returned safely. At the time, we carried rope in the trunks of our cars, and I thought, "Well, this is what it's for." The rope in the trunk of our radio car was needed for this call.

You've Heard of Snakes on a Plane

Anyone who really knows me knows that I really don't like snakes. I will walk a mile out of my way to avoid seeing or going near one. Corpus Christi Catholic Church was having its annual fair on a weekend in mid-June in the early eighties. I was assigned to regular patrol for area B, the Long Hill side of town. A call came in from a resident on Susan Drive that she had a snake in her garage. My first thought was, "What the hell am I going to do?"

Again, this situation was not covered in any of the training we had received. Remember, I came from Union, New Jersey, which was not the country. After some quick thinking on my part, I remembered that one of our special officers was working the fair. I quickly rode over to the fair and asked him to come with me. On our way, I told him about the call. He said it was no problem. We arrived, and, sure enough, the longest snake I've ever seen was partially curled up on the garage floor. Fortunately, the homeowner stayed in the house after we arrived and didn't see the frightened look on my face. Bill, the special officer, went right over to the snake and, with the help of a shovel, managed to get him in a plastic garbage can. Next we had to transport this snake back to the swamp. Luckily for us, the garbage can had a lid. Bill and the garbage can that held the snake were in the backseat of my patrol vehicle. I rode quickly to Meyersville Road, which had one of the swamp's many entrances. I opened the car door, and Bill took out the garbage pail. He lifted the lid, and the snake slithered out of the can and back to the swamp where he belonged.

"Doe, a deer, a female deer..."

While working the day shift, our dispatcher received a call from the Fairmount Country Club that one of their front bay windows was broken and that there was glass and blood all over. I responded and met the manager; we conducted a brief search of the immediate area. We located deer fur by the window and immediately thought that a deer had run into the window and broken the glass. A few minutes later, we located a deer wandering in one of the hallways. How were we going to get this deer out of the building when the dining room area was about to open? Most of the dining room was surrounded by glass windows, and our concern was that the deer might take out another window. I opened the double glass doors leading to the parking lot, and after coaxing the deer, she finally left the building and ran across Southern Boulevard toward the Great Swamp.

Green Village Deli

Years ago, the Green Village Deli was called Botti's, which was more of a butcher shop with a few groceries for sale. Eventually, it was sold to a family. The husband and wife ran the store, and their three girls helped out from time to time. The husband worked full-time as a paid fireman in Essex County and ran the store during his off-hours. The deli was always a place for good conversation and good coffee. Most of our officers enjoyed the owners company and conversation. They were good people. They eventually sold the business and last I heard moved out west to Arizona. In all of my years on the police force, we were never called there for any police-related incident.

Fairmount County Deli: Harry

One of the first gentlemen I met as a member of the Chatham Township Police Force was Harry from the Fairmount Avenue Deli. I first met Harry in 1977. His deli was the only one on that side of town. The store hours were 6:00 a.m. to 8:00 or 9:00 pm, and Harry always had a smiling face for his customers. His wife Mary worked there as well. The deli had an old-fashioned counter and a few tables. There was another section of picnic tables that were made out of lumber from Vermont. Harry also sold a few groceries as well as milk and eggs. I didn't realize that Harry had been the mayor of Chatham years before I was hired and was still pretty influential in the town. He pulled no punches, either.

Harry used to close the store on Sundays, but after we became friends, he told me I was welcome to come in anytime I saw his car. Sometimes we sat and talked, mostly about his property in Vermont. Little did we know that one day I, too, would buy a house in Vermont. I think because of him my wife and I traveled to Vermont and immediately fell in love with the state. Eventually, Harry and Mary sold their business and really retired. Unfortunately, I was on the medical call for the first of Harry's serious health issues, and he passed away a few years after he retired.

Dealing with the Crazies

There has to be some truth to the full moon theory. Whenever there is a full moon, police receive a high number of crazy-type calls and have to deal with a larger number of difficult situations. On some full moon evenings, we would get a call from a woman who thought that someone was watching her through her windows and that people were at her door. I know that it sounds like a legitimate call that police officers should respond to. But when you have received this type of call often enough, and the situation has always turned out all right, you begin to put less faith in the legitimacy of the call. We still had to respond and investigate, but it could become a nuisance. After the perimeter of the house had been checked, we would resume patrol, especially as the homeowner did not want us to come into her home. She did not want an officer physically to approach her door in case the Russians were watching her home. This woman did not live alone but with her husband and children. One evening she called several times to indicate that the Russians had leaked some type of gas into her house and that although she was all right, she wanted us to keep an extra eye out. Another night she called back and claimed someone was at her door again. Another time someone else was at her door, and even though she couldn't identify him or her, she just knew her or she was after her. After the second or third such call, we watched the house for awhile. It should be noted that most of her calls took place during a full moon. While we were watching her house, she again called the station and reported the same type of incident. We explained to her that no one was at her house. The detectives spoke to her and her husband and expressed our concern for her well-being and the safety of others in her home. The calls stopped for a few months but soon resumed again, and each time we assured her that everything was all right. As a police officer, you still had to respond to the residence and reassure them that everything was all right. To my knowledge, she was never hospitalized for any mental condition.

Our calls for service always seemed to increase when there was a full moon. People locked themselves out of their houses or cars far more frequently during a full moon. One day we received a medical aid call from a motorist who was sitting in his vehicle and not feeling well. Upon my arrival, I found the driver banging his head against the steering wheel. At first glance, you could tell that there was an emotional issue. He refused medical transport, so I just talked him to a calmer state, and he was on his way. Little did I know that this event would occur almost every other month. The motorist, whom we will call George, worked at a prestigious research company in the area and frequented the Madison Bowling Alley. It turned out that the Madison and Summit Police Departments were all too familiar with him, and this behavior had been going on for years. The situation became particularly more difficult whenever George pulled over near a school, around which school-age children were present. We would have to try to reason with him. He wasn't there to look at the children, but you have to remember that around this time Adam Walsh was kidnapped and killed in Florida. People were, in general, very cautious. Often, if someone pulled over by a school to eat his lunch or to have a snack, onlookers became very paranoid and would call the police about a suspicious vehicle. But what do you consider a suspicious vehicle?

Spouses and Significant Others and Their Influence

I remember our first police department Christmas party, which was the first real time that our wives got to meet each other. It was a squad party, which usually only included that squad's members and their spouses. Later on, it became a bigger event that more officers could attend. As a rookie without any aspirations at the time to move up in rank, I found it interesting to see the politicking involved. Some people laughed at awful jokes, and others patted each other on the backs, when in reality they could care less. Don't misunderstand me: the holiday parties were a great time, and some of the humor and interactions were quite genuine. As a general rule, though, these parties were better when promotions were not in the near future.

Very seldom did spouses come to visit the police headquarters. The wife of one of our chiefs used to work at the tax office, and it was always pleasant to see and speak with her. I never really realized the influence that the officers' wives had until I worked for a particular sergeant early in my career. He was a great guy off the job, but at work the Wyatt Earp Syndrome came out. Though he was all smiles in the locker room while we dressed for duty, as soon as the police uniform was on he transformed into Joe Friday: "Just the facts, ma'am." At times he had the personality of Dr. Jekyll and Mr. Hyde. When he received another promotion to lieutenant, he became nearly impossible to work with. We actually had officers leave our department because they saw no future with this particular officer.

One day, I was working directly for him in another unit, and I had had enough of the condescending way he spoke to me. This particular day after my shift, I went into his office to clear the air. I told him that I was not the enemy and did not appreciate being spoken to in a condescending tone. If this was going to continue, then I wanted a transfer back to a squad. This incident did clear the air; we shook hands and started over fresh the next day. During his career, several police officers went into the chief's office to complain about him. The best complaint resulted from how difficult it was to receive time off. If the members of his squad wanted to take time off, we had to follow procedure and put in a request. For example, if I had a wedding or a family event that I wanted to attend, I would submit the request, but his approval took a very long time to receive. One day, I asked him when my request was going to get approved. He had the nerve to tell me that he had to check with his then-girlfriend whether it was all right. "What?" I thought. "Are you kidding me?" You see, he was in the midst of a divorce and had to check with his girlfriend whether they had plans before granting any of his officers time off. Basically, the officers who worked with him during those years were made to feel as though they were part of his divorce proceedings.

This was a practice that continued with everyone who worked with him until the Police Benevolent Association changed the language in the contract. From that time forward, vacation and time off requests were based on seniority. This particular person worked with a lot of senior officers, and he often complained to the chief that although he was the sergeant in charge of the shift, the others had time off picks over him. The next PBA contract was changed to reflect that rank had first pick and seniority second. He continued to go through marital issues, and it certainly felt like we were all going through them, too. A wise senior officer once told me that you could always learn something from someone no matter who you worked with. Indeed, whenever I worked for someone like that sergeant, I learned a great deal, mostly how not to treat people. But this man also had a lot of great qualities, and I think if his personal situation had been better, he would have been easier to work with.

I found it odd that the only other time we would see some of the officers' wives was on payday. They knew the exact time that our checks were delivered to headquarters, and they wanted to cash the check and pay their bills. I guess they couldn't wait until their husband got home. You have to keep in mind that most police officers in the early seventies and eighties lived in the community where they worked. At the time, I was the only officer who lived out of town, and no, my wife didn't drive up to receive my check. When automatic deposit began, it saved officers from coming in on their days off to pick up their checks.

Then we had the officer who was single and dating. Just when we got to know her name, the officer would decide he didn't like her or want to date her any longer. It became quite comical after a while. If a female motorist happened to be pulled over for a minor motor vehicle infraction, and if during the brief conversation between her and the officer he discovered that she was single, there was an excellent chance he would ask her out or invite himself over for dinner if she lived in town. Some motorists and residents made complaints, which were dealt with confidentially. These incidents were few in number and never occurred when another officer was present.

Delivering Sad News

Probably one of the most difficult parts of being a police officer was delivering sad news. Sad news could be anything from informing people that a member of their family had been seriously injured in a car accident to informing them that a vacation home had been burglarized or lost to a natural disaster. One night on patrol when I was still fairly new to the department, the desk sergeant called one of the other patrol officers and asked him to code 10-81, which meant to go to the private channel on the radio. The joke was that everyone in town could still hear it on their scanners. The sergeant gave an address, and the officer was to notify the residents that one of their children, a son in his late teens, had been killed in a motor vehicle accident in Maine. A phone number and contact person were provided. The officer given this assignment responded back to the sergeant, "Send college boy, too"; it would be good training. So the sergeant called college boy—me—and asked me to meet the other officer and assist.

It was around 2:00 a.m. when I responded to the call. This particular house had no lights on. I met the other officer, who had at least twenty years of experience yet still wanted the new guy with him. No one really likes or enjoys these types of assignments, but because the phone was not in service, there was no other way to notify the parents. Ringing the doorbell did not produce the desired results, but loudly banging on the door finally worked. The father came to the door with his wife at his side. We asked if we could come in, and of course they were worried. I asked if there was a place where we could all sit down and talk. All of a sudden this call became personal because of the effect this news was going to have on them. "This news is going to be very stressful for the family," I told myself.

We didn't know the family history, such as whether the boy had any siblings. First, we had to verify that the couple had a son who was in Maine, his last location, and a full description of his appearance. We knew from the identification found on the individual in Maine that he was their son, but we still wanted to verify this information. We asked if there were clergy members whom we could call or another family member whom we could contact to assist them. The parents informed us that they would be all right and thanked us for the compassion we had shown. We offered any assistance they might have needed to get through the next few days. We stayed with the family for an hour or two, and we assured them that we would keep an eye on the house for them while they traveled out of state.

Back at headquarters we had a book that was called the day book. The day book was where officers would write notes to the oncoming shifts and make them aware of various developments throughout the town. The day book substituted for an official roll call. Roll call was when the shift supervisor went over the events of the day or evening prior to the start of a shift. This was one of those incidents that we had to record in the book so that the following shifts would know what had happened and that they should keep an extra eye on the family's residence.

Isn't that just Ducky

I was only on the police department a few months when I remember receiving a call from the dispatcher stating a neighbor on Van Houton Avenue called reporting a Duck was waddling back and forth by a storm drain and was afraid for it. I also remember it was on a weekend for reasons you will know soon enough. When I arrived, sure enough the Mama Duck (Hen) was waddling back and forth on top of the sewer drain. Upon further inspection, I discovered six ducklings down in the sewer drain. By this time, several neighbors had wandered over and wondered how were we going to reunite the ducklings with their mother.

I made the decision to have our dispatcher call out the on call person from our Department of Public Works. In about 15 minutes or so, the public works person arrived and within minutes was able to lift the sewer drain cover and hand me the ducklings and reunite them with their mother.

The story does not quite end there. The next day, which was Monday, the Superintendent of Public Works contacted our police department and I'm sure he spoke to a lieutenant or above and wondered why he had an overtime slip from one of his workers for rescuing baby ducks on a Sunday. You can imagine my surprise when I was called into the patrol lieutenant's office and asked about it. I was informed that if this should happen again, the ducks would find a way out on their own. Yes, the town had to pay the overtime.

Someone with Too Much Time on His Hands

All municipalities and cities have parking issues and complaints. Chatham Township is comprised mostly of paved, tree-lined, one-family homes, most of which have manicured lawns. I'm sure every now and then we all have parked on the wrong side of the street or have parked facing the wrong way. We once had a gentleman who would ride around town and call us to make a complaint whenever he found a vehicle that was not facing the right way. An officer was then required to go to the residence of the affected party and ask him or her to either move the car or receive a summons.

Because of their proximity to Shunpike Road and NJ Transit Service into the city, some of our streets have two- or four-hour parking limits. The two- to four-hour limit was imposed because we had a few residents and non-residents who would park off Noe Avenue and walk to Shunpike to take the bus into the city to work. People didn't want to see a car parked in front of their house all day, so they would call to complain. The previously mentioned gentleman called on average two to three times a week about these vehicles. It didn't matter if they were landscapers or tree servicemen or others working nearby. This gentleman appeared to be on a personal mission, which lasted over a period of months. He would even come in and visit with our chief. Finally, the chief had enough and called me into his office. I was a patrol sergeant at the time, and he asked if I would go over and meet with this individual to try to calm things down. I would later serve as the Henry Kissinger for quite a few incidents that the chief wanted handled diplomatically. This particular case boiled down to the chief being tired of dealing with this man and wanting someone else to deal with him. I met with this individual a few times, and though he was rather pleasant, he had a different view on parking. The situation eventually calmed down after we devoted less attention to him, as we should have done in the first place.

One of our officers was actually reprimanded after this gentleman was observed looking inside the officer's patrol vehicle with a camera. When this individual was asked why he had been looking in the officer's vehicle, he denied it. When the officer heard this report, he responded to the gentleman's home to inquire about what he had done. Apparently, the officer wasn't supposed to go to his home and question him. This gentleman also used to take pictures of our patrol vehicles at one of our malls while the officers were on break . He would send the pictures to our chief. This automatically required an investigation into who the officers were and why their vehicles were there. Most of the time, the officers were on break or picking up their lunches and were always subject to call. His calls were a complete waste of time and taxpayer money.

Was It the Garbage Man?

At one point our town experienced a few nighttime burglaries, which were rare in a community where most of the residents were home in the evening. One particular summer evening in the late eighties, I was dispatched to a residential burglary. I was a detective at the time. I heard the call being dispatched to the patrol, who respond first. A detective is then usually called to process the scene and conduct a more detailed investigation. I remember it was around 10:00 p.m. when I received the call, and the caller thought the suspect or suspects were still in the area. The patrol at the scene discovered a piece of clothing—physical evidence—that could be used to track the suspect. It just so happened that that evening police dispatcher Kathy Finnerman was working in New Providence. She had a bloodhound and had worked on her days off with sheriff's officers and their dogs on detecting and tracking individuals. We called over to New Providence Police, and Kathy responded with her dog. We went searching through the woods for the suspect. The suspect must have heard us coming through the woods because a patrol officer in the area observed him running and apprehended him. The individual apprehended was shirtless at the time and had scratches over his face and arms. We struggled on the ground while trying to detain him. He was arrested and transported to police headquarters. Our municipal judge was notified and set bail, which is the protocol for an indictable offense. When filling out bail forms, one of the questions besides where you reside concerns the arrested person's employment. He mentioned a trash company, and after further questioning he revealed that he had known the residents would be away on vacation for the week. He hadn't known that the residents would be coming home that night. He also admitted to us that he was not alone, but he was not going to give up his accomplice. He was indicted on burglary and possession of burglary tools. He pleaded guilty at trial and, because he had prior burglary and drug charges, received a sentence of five to seven years.

Suicides and Accidental Shooting

In my career, I have not seen any two families handle sad news the same way. I have had to tell loved ones that their significant others or children have taken their own lives. I remember one particular call when a woman came home and discovered her husband in their basement; he had been shot and appeared to be dead. Upon our arrival, we discovered the weapon still locked in his hand after he had fired a bullet into his own head. Because the gun was still clutched in his hand with his finger by the trigger, we had to make sure the gun was safe and would not go off again. The police had to treat it as a crime scene until proven otherwise. There was blood and brain matter spattered on the wall in the basement. In an adjacent office, I discovered a note typed on an old-fashioned typewriter that said he couldn't take the pain anymore; the money was running out, he didn't know what to do or how to pay his bills, and he risked losing his home. He couldn't do that to his wife. The man, our victim, was in his mid to late sixties and had had cancer for a number of years. The note went on to say that he had recently learned that the cancer had metastasized.

If I can digress for a moment, this incident took place after I had been a police officer for a number of years. In those years I had been on hundreds of first aid calls, some minor ones but also some more serious ones in which the person had passed away. I've seen my share of how families suffer when a loved one passes away. As police officers and often the first responders, we did everything in our power to administer the proper first aid and basic life support until a more competent medical team arrived. These teams included the first aid squad and medics from either Overlook Hospital or Morristown Memorial.

There was one week I remember very clearly. It took place in the late eighties before I was promoted to sergeant. I had five medical emergencies that resulted in five DOAs, or dead on arrivals. The causes were massive stroke, heart attack, or passed away suddenly in their sleep. All of these incidents occurred during a five-night period that was shortly before Christmas. It was awful, and I really felt for the families.

To return to the call regarding the man in the basement, I informed his wife that he may have been cleaning his weapon and that it appeared to have been an accidental shooting death. The couple had been married for many years, and it was very painful to see her suffer the loss of her longtime spouse. The typed note was taken as evidence and never shown to the family; they are not customarily shared. One could speculate that he had taken his own life or, as I suggested to his wife, that he may have gone into the basement to clean his weapon. We'll never know for sure, but we do know there was no foul play or criminal activity involved. I'm not too sure how other officers handled these types of calls, but I'm sure they did so with compassion, as they should have. These types of calls were always painful. But as police officers, we had to be the pillars of strength for the victims' families, even at the scenes of horrific traffic accidents where multiple victims were crying out in pain. The police had to reassure the victims that they would be all right. The police had to control the scene.

Another call I encountered was a murder-suicide of a husband and wife. A call came in from one of their children that they had not heard from their parents in a few days (according to the neighbors, it was more like a few weeks).

They also called a neighbor, who went to the home and saw their vehicles. But there was no sign of anyone moving around, and the mail had been accumulating in the mailbox. After we gained entry to the residence, a plastic bag was found securely fastened over the wife's head, and the husband had taken his own life by overdosing on medication. These two had been inseparable and had done everything together. When I was on patrol I used to stop by and talk with them while they raked leaves or cut their lawn. They were one of the few families in town who didn't have a landscaper or a lawn service. After speaking with the family, we learned that the man's wife had Alzheimer's and that he was riddled with cancer. Their family had never known the extent of their illnesses as they resided on the West Coast and rarely visited.

One Saturday night I was working in the Traffic Safety Unit from 6:00 p.m. to 2:00 a.m. I was on patrol a little past 7:00 pm, and it was still light out. All of a sudden, a call came over the radio to respond to headquarters immediately because of an incident in our parking lot. I remember the evening as clear and warm, in late spring.

How do I remember the weather? On my patrol vehicle sheet, I wrote the dates and times of our calls, and I always listed the weather in case I was called into court and needed the description for recollection. My shift had just started when the frantic call came over the radio from the dispatcher. Subsequently, it was discovered that a male in his mid-twenties had driven into the police department parking lot, parked his vehicle, exited, and shot himself in the head with a revolver. The young male was pronounced dead at the scene. We discovered his identity through the vehicle registration. His parents later told us that he had been having emotional issues. Our police chaplain assisted the family during this very difficult time.

Too Young

When I was first assigned to the detective bureau in the late eighties, there were two detectives. One handled juveniles and the other handled criminal investigations, which also included evidence and property clerk duties. I had just put the key in the lock of my office door when I received a call from our dispatcher about the possible suicide of a juvenile in the Wickham Woods Section of town. I responded to the scene along with the detective lieutenant and discovered a white male, fifteen years of age, who was unresponsive and cyanotic. This young man was the second of three children. The oldest son was away at college, and the other two lived at home and were still in high school. Part of the investigation included interviews with possible witnesses, parents, friends, and acquaintances so as to discover the motive. At first this case was determined to be an unattended death, and we were suspicious at first.

The victim was found in his underwear without shirt or shoes and was found in close proximity to the doorknob. Due to how the body and clothing were discovered, it was later determined that the cause of death was autoerotic asphyxiation or breath control play, which is the intentional restriction of oxygen to the brain for the purpose of sexual arousal. This determination was made with the assistance of the Medical Examiner's Office and the Morris County Prosecutor's Office, which investigates all unattended deaths to determine if foul play has taken place. In autoerotic asphyxiation various methods are used to achieve the level of oxygen depletion needed and include hanging, suffocation, and self-strangulation with a ligature. Sometimes complicated devices are used to produce the desired effects, but not in this case. The practice can be dangerous even if performed with care, as evident in this case. Autoerotic asphyxiation may often be mistaken for suicide, which is a major cause of death in teenagers. Our preliminary investigation revealed that this particular teenager had had enormous pressure on him from his family and friends. Extensive interviews were conducted, and at first the death was thought to have been a suicide. Only after several weeks was it determined to have been an accidental death. Our school system was alerted, and they had additional counselors ready to deal with students who may have been having a difficult time coping. We were hopeful that other teens would not engage in this activity.

Not Such a Good Friday

I remember well a particular Good Friday when I worked in the detective bureau. My day shift had just started when we received a call of a hanging at a residence on Fairmount Avenue. The caller was the deceased person's mother. She had gone shopping earlier in the morning and after arriving home had seen a light on in the garage. She had walked into the garage and found her son hanging. Patrol units were the first ones to arrive on the scene and attempted to revive the man, but it was too late. Cyanosis had begun to develop and reviving efforts were futile.

During an initial investigation of this type, officers have to check for any evidence of foul play. It is considered a crime scene until determined otherwise. There is no prescribed amount of time because the investigation can lead you in different ways. A local clergyman was called to the scene to be with the family. As with all unattended deaths in our county, the prosecutor's office has to be notified and responds. They don't take over the investigation, but they do offer assistance and make calls to the medical examiner. When the medical examiner arrives, the scene is gone over again, and basic information is provided. It is only when the medical examiner says the body can be moved that the body is transported to either a hospital or a funeral home.

Later that same day, I had finally gotten back to headquarters and my office around 3:30 p.m. when the dispatcher called with a possible accidental shooting at a residence off Green Village Road. The patrol officers who first responded determined that the individual involved was deceased. I responded to the residence and was led to the upstairs bathroom where the deceased, a male in his mid-twenties, had been found lying on the bathroom floor. The bathroom window was open, and the storm window was partially up; a rifle lay alongside his body. The weapon (a short-barreled rifle) was secured as evidence and photographs were taken according to standard operating procedure.

After a rather lengthy discussion with his family members, it was determined that he enjoyed shooting rabbits and other small wild animals out this window. Hunting or discharging a firearm was not permitted in the township except during hunting season. This particular property abutted the Great Swamp, but many people don't realize that bullets can travel a great distance and be deadly, as in this case. Sometimes I would watch the news and see people in Middle Eastern countries shooting weapons into the air in celebration. I don't think they understood that the same bullets being shot into the air had to come back to the ground and could injure or kill someone. It was later determined through evidence collected at the scene that this was indeed an accidental shooting death caused by the trajectory of the bullet. I was able to conclude this investigation around midnight. It was a long day for me but a far longer one for the families of the victims. Over time, working cases such as the ones mentioned here affects police and first responders physically and emotionally.

Humor and Pranks on the Job

We all need a little humor in our lives, and the same principle applies to police work. Down times on the job were the perfect occasions to have fun. Most of the fun times occurred on the midnight shift. A typical shift used to consist of a civilian police dispatcher, a sergeant, and three or four patrol officers; we were sometimes supplemented by the traffic unit officer and usually by one or two detectives. On more than one occasion when we were training new dispatchers, we told them a ghost story called "The Ghost of Ray." Ray had been the first name of an officer who had suffered a fatal heart attack while at work in police headquarters. In December 1977, Ray was working the day shift and had just come in for his coffee break around 9:30 a.m. While standing at the command desk reading the blotter (or day's events), Ray collapsed and was later pronounced dead. For the prank, one of the officers kept the dispatcher busy with manuals and procedures while another officer tied and secured fishing line to our front public entrance doors, which were all glass from top to bottom. Afterwards, the officer would go around to our ground-level windows and come into the building undetected. He had to crank out the window, which was left unlocked on purpose, and remove the screen so he could climb inside.

Part of the joke was the use of minimum lighting in the building. Because it was 2:00 or 3:00 a.m., the building was empty and there was no need for all of the lights to be on. So the bank of lights for the hallways would be turned off, and the officer who was training the dispatcher would leave and announce that he'd be back in a few hours. Not long after the training officer had left the building, the front door would open and shut on its own about four or five times. First, the door would open a little, and then one of the doors to the conference room would slam shut. Another officer was remotely opening the front doors while simultaneously calling in on almost all the phone lines. Eventually, the dispatcher would call the sergeant on the radio and ask him to come to headquarters right away. This would go on a little while longer until we would finally tell the dispatcher what had actually happened. Even after the police dispatchers knew it had been a joke, they still kept on all the lights in the building. I wonder why?

Other pranks included calling the desk and identifying ourselves as the Morris County Fog Commission. We would ask the person taking the call to please notify the officers that we would be out observing and taking fog samples to determine fog levels. Nash Field used to be flooded with water in the wintertime so that children in town could ice-skate. Well, you probably know where this is going, but someone would always call in June, July, or August to ask if there was any ice-skating. Of course, this call would go to new dispatchers or patrol officers assigned to the desk. Though the town's recreation center had a direct number to call to find out if there was ice-skating, and though the public was repeatedly asked not to call police headquarters about ice-skating, they still did. There was even a huge plywood sign in front of the field that indicated whether there was ice-skating.

Speaking of calling police headquarters, it also didn't matter how many newspaper announcements or local radio spots we placed to warn the public against tying up emergency lines by calling police headquarters; residents still called. On more than one occasion, I was assigned to the desk and inundated with callers asking when their power was coming back on. Finally I said, "Wait a minute, let me turn yours on now for you." Of course, I didn't have that capability. "Call the power company," I generally told those who called us. "And let them know so they can send a crew to repair. The police cannot turn your power on or off, sorry."

As I mentioned earlier, my first squad assignment was with my training officer Richard and another officer who had a very distinct German accent. He was a very good officer, lived in town, and raised his family there. Back then we used to pick up the officers who lived in town for duty. So five minutes before the shift ended, we had to pick up the officers who lived in town and would be relieving us. This particular officer lived on the Long Hill side of town, which was a good five minutes away from headquarters where my vehicle was parked. One day, one of the more seasoned officers I worked with said, "When you pick him up today, ask him if the flag he's displaying on the flag pole next to the U.S. flag is a flag of East Germany or West Germany." Later that day I picked up this officer, and as soon as he got in the car, I asked the question. "What do you mean?" he replied, in the thickest German accent I've ever heard. The rant continued for the whole ride back to headquarters. I never asked again, but whenever a new officer was hired, we made sure he or she asked him the same question. It was a good way to start the shift with a positive note.

For our vertically challenged officers, phone books or wooden blocks were often helpfully placed in their cars to help them to see over the steering wheel or to reach the gas and brake pedals—as a joke, of course. We also had other jokers who would turn the heater up high in July and August so that a certain officer would really "feel the heat"; they would turn up the air conditioning in the wintertime. Little things like these pranks really helped us get through shifts.

"Thou shalt not take others people's goods out of the refrigerator." Now, just because you forgot to bring your meal and either didn't have the money to buy food or couldn't find an open restaurant in town, you still didn't have the right to take someone else's food. We only had a few officers who actually examined the lunch bags in the fridge, but if they liked what they saw, they would eat it.

This thievery only lasted a little while because after eating something that contained a laxative, the lunch thefts stopped. Did I mention that we sometimes used to tie a rubber band to the water spray in the kitchen so that when the time came to add water to the coffee pot...you got it, they got sprayed. I was never a victim of this prank, but I know a few officers who had fingerprint ink placed on the brims of their hats. Guess what happened when they put those hats on!

This next story is comical now, but it wasn't at the time, I'm sure. The chief's secretary office was next to his office, and one day a high-ranking officer appeared to be having a diabetic attack. The secretary went to her office and actually dialed 911 when she could have just walked ten steps to the command desk. There was also an officer who stopped a car for a moving violation and then proceeded back to his patrol car to write the summons. It began to rain very hard, and the officer beeped his horn for the driver to come back to his patrol vehicle to receive his summons. (You can't make this stuff up)

Right Place at the Right Time

My wife and I had just brought our first child home from the hospital on April 15, 1979. I was on patrol in a residential area off of Shunpike Road when the dispatcher gave me a call of a child not breathing. As the address was being stated to me via the radio, I realized I was directly in front of the house; as a result, I responded in seconds. I raced in with the oxygen unit and took the baby in my arms. I repositioned the head, and the baby began to breathe on his own. There was no need for the oxygen unit, though the first aid squad also responded quickly. The baby was only a few months old. You could tell the first-time parents were extremely nervous and worried but managed to calm down once they knew their child was fine. The baby and his parents were transported to Overlook Hospital for further observation. Later that evening I stopped back at the house to make sure everyone was doing well.

Gunman Running Through a Store

Chatham Township has two malls: Hickory Square Shopping Center and the Chatham Mall. This one particular Saturday afternoon, headquarters received a call of a man with a gun running into the Source of Sounds, a record store in the Hickory Mall. There was only one record store at the mall, and it was on Green Village Road. I responded to the scene while another officer was en route. When I arrived, people outside indicated that the gunman had run into the back of the store. I got everyone out of the store and with my gun drawn entered the storage area. As I entered the storage area, a male about six feet tall with a medium build was brandishing a revolver, which appeared to be a .38 caliber handgun. I repeatedly ordered him to drop the gun, but he kept holding it; at the same time, my backup arrived with his weapon drawn. I could see out of the corner of my eye that his weapon was drawn and ready to fire. The gunman was raising the gun in our direction, and at the same time we were yelling "Drop it, drop it!" He finally lowered the gun and had a grin on his face like this was all a joke. He dropped the gun and was handcuffed and transported to headquarters. Upon closer examination of the weapon, it was determined to be a .38 caliber prop used in a high school play. He had brought it to show his friends who worked at the store. The gunman turned out to be a high school senior. He was charged and eventually appeared before a juvenile judge. The sad part was that this juvenile and his mother both thought the situation was a joke and that we, the police, had made something out of nothing. In court the judge made a point of telling the juvenile and his mother that these officers would have been justified in shooting him because of the gun in his hand, especially given that he had been aiming it at officers. The juvenile received sixty hours of community service, and the judge talked rather sternly to the mother. I went home that night thinking that the day could have gone in a very different and tragic direction.

Burglary Suspects Apprehended

Police officers in general will seldom apprehend burglars in the act, and those who work in Chatham Township rarely encounter burglars; this occurrence might happen once in a career. I was fortunate enough to catch two of them in the act of committing a crime. During my tenure as a police officer, individuals from outside of our county committed most of our burglaries. Most burglaries in our community and similar areas were committed during the daylight hours when people were at work.

But one occasion I encountered was different. Monday Night Football was just ending, and I was on patrol on Green Village Road when a call came in that a resident on Spring Valley Road had just encountered someone breaking into her home while she was present. The caller, a female, stated that her husband had been asleep on the couch downstairs when she had heard glass break. She was frightened, and she and her children were upstairs. I arrived at the house within seconds. As I approached the residence I saw the front door ajar and the windowpane closest to the door lock broken. There were traces of blood on the door as well as the glass. There was no time to wait for backup because that officer was responding from the other side of town.

As I entered the home, I discovered the homeowner sleeping on the couch with the television still on. I then spotted two individuals, one male and one female and both in their twenties. They were standing in the dining room with silverware in their hands and startled looks on their faces. On the dining room table was a wooden flatware chest. My weapon was drawn, and I ordered both individuals to get on the ground. The male had signs of bleeding on his right hand, and the woman wore an old army-style jacket, the kind you can purchase from army and navy surplus stores. A pat down of the female resulted in discovering silverware, which had the same pattern as the pieces in the flatware chest.

Once the two were arrested and secured, I yelled up to the second floor that it was okay for her to come down. The woman came downstairs, woke up her husband, and enlightened him on the night's activities. Both of the arrested individuals were transported to headquarters to be charged and processed for burglary. While talking to them later, they indicated that they were both from Morristown. They had decided to walk down South Street and onto Spring Valley Road so they could find a house to break into. The male defendant blamed the idea on his female companion, and the female defendant blamed him. Both were transported to the Morris County Jail, and bail was set at $10,000 with no 10 percent. Prior to trial, both parties pled guilty and were sentenced to one to three years with a fine assessed. Both individuals had prior arrests for burglaries.

The Drug Store Has the Best Drug.

False alarms can be set off because of weather conditions, power outages or surges, or even human error. People may have entered the wrong code, or a business could have changed the code without informing its employees (don't laugh, it's happened). This one particular Sunday morning, headquarters received a burglary alarm at a pharmacy in the Chatham Mall. I was dispatched and responded, and another patrol car was also responding. The other officer was going to take the front of the store, and I went to check the back door. I pulled my radio car up to the back door and noticed it was ajar. I radioed that information to headquarters and to the other unit responding. The time of the alarm was not when the employees usually came in, either. The officer who was at the front of the store saw a pane of glass missing, and we were confident we had someone inside.

Then, at that moment, I was confronted with a male who was attempting to run out the back door. Between me and my patrol vehicle, though, there was no way he could escape. He had in his possession numerous bottles of a controlled dangerous substance (CDS). He was arrested and transported to headquarters for processing. A search warrant was obtained, and a subsequent search of his vehicle, which was discovered in the rear parking lot, revealed numerous maps with particular locations circled strewn about the car. After interviewing the suspect, he admitted to breaking into not only our pharmacy but also fifteen others in the area and a few in Bergen County. All the affected agencies were advised, and retainers placed him at the county jail. The retainers ensured that if he made bail on our charges, he wouldn't be released until he had satisfied the other municipalities' pending charges. The arrested individual was remanded to the county jail. Subsequently, he was indicted and pled guilty. He was sentenced to five to seven years, fined, and ordered to take part in a drug rehabilitation program.

Bicyclists Beware

One of the officers on my squad when I was a patrol sergeant had more energy than anyone I knew. He would go all day and night stopping cars and checking on suspicious vehicles or suspicious persons. From the moment this particular midnight shift started to the moment it ended, we were running with calls. As soon as I had sat down to do my paperwork and review all the night's reports, this officer, whom I'll call Bob, spotted a bicyclist riding on Southern Boulevard near the Presbyterian church. The bicyclist had no light or warning device on either the front or back of the bike. The officer stopped the bicyclist and discovered that he had no identification on him. When he searched the leather pouch on the back of the bike for some form of identification, a controlled dangerous substance (CDS) was found. The individual was arrested and processed at headquarters. A sample of the CDS found was tested with a CDS identification kit, and it was determined to be cocaine.

One More for the Road

One of my philosophies of policing was education. After I had conducted a motor vehicle stop and informed the driver of the infraction, I could tell whether the driver understood what he or she had done wrong. There will always be drivers who can't wait for the police to arrive at their doors and ask, "What did I do wrong?" or "What did you stop me for?" Trust me, I've heard them all. Thinking back to my rookie year, I remember the patrol lieutenant telling me, "Son, if you can, give someone a break." He always emphasized the residents, and I knew why. I went a step further and replied, "Why don't I treat everyone the same way?" He liked my comeback.

The word discretion is a noun and generally means the quality of behaving or speaking in such a way as to avoid causing offense or revealing private information; it also means the freedom to decide what should be done in a particular case. Police officers use discretion every day. There are, of course, certain crimes and offenses in which officers do not have the luxury of discretion, but in minor incidents and many traffic offenses, they do. As officers, we sometimes observed a vehicle slightly weaving, making very wide turns, or impeding the flow of traffic in a manner that indicated the driver or operator was impaired to a degree. The impairment was usually due to the consumption of too much alcohol. Ninety-nine percent of the drivers I stopped and asked whether they had been drinking answered yes, and when asked how many drinks they had had to drink, the answer was always two beers! Even if they had drunk only one or as many as six, I think they were programmed to say two beers.

Years ago officers could stop someone, and assuming the driver lived in town, they could ask him or her to park the car in exchange for a ride home. This practice remained in place until our county adopted a zero-tolerance policy for drunk drivers, which removed our discretion. But when officers did have discretion regarding drunk drivers, they would drop off the driver and tell him or her to retrieve his or her keys at headquarters the next day. If there was a next time, that person might not be so fortunate.

Now, this courtesy didn't happen every day, nor did it happen if a driver was involved in an accident or some other altercation. I remember in the early eighties I had a driver park his vehicle on Rolling Hill Drive, and I took him home to the Wickham Woods section of town. This incident happened between 2:00 and 2:30 a.m. No sooner had I dropped off the driver than I observed him walking down Southern Boulevard toward his vehicle. I stopped him and asked what he was doing as it was now only 3:00 a.m. He said that he felt rested and was now fine to drive. What had happened was that when he had gotten home, he had taken the spare set of car keys with him because we had held onto the original set of keys. I told him, "If you get in that car and drive, you will be arrested." He did enter the vehicle, and as soon as he started it, I arrested him and charged him with DWI. I remember he refused to take the Breathalyzer; this refusal meant another summons. A few months later, I had to testify in court to his impairment. The judge not only found him guilty and gave him a large fine but also told him that he should have listened to the officer. But as a result of the directive from the Morris County Prosecutor's Office in the late eighties, this courtesy was discontinued. For more information, I suggest reading about John's Law, which was enacted in 2001; it deals with confiscating the vehicle of a drunk driver. Personally, I agree with the new law and directives from the Morris County Prosecutor's Office.

Nighttime Swim–Skinny Dipping, Anyone?

Who among us doesn't like to go swimming on a hot summer night? Maybe the air conditioner isn't working at home, or you want to cool off with your family or friends. It may sound like a great idea, but what if neither you nor your friends own a pool? I found out what a few teenagers decided to do one hot summer evening around 12:30 a.m, when I was dispatched to a residence on Meyersville Road. The caller was a resident who reported hearing sounds and noises coming from his pool. Most of the properties on Meyersville Road are long and deep. The pool in question was quite a distance from the home. I pulled up to a neighbor's yard and walked over to the pool, but I didn't see anyone splashing around. The pool did have a few ripples, but I thought they had perhaps come from the pool filter. Just as I was looking over the edge of the pool, which was above ground and not fenced in, a guy and a girl jumped out of the water. They swam to the other side rather quickly and ran off toward the Great Swamp, which backed up to this property. They were only wearing their birthday suits and must have been holding their breaths for a while. They scared the hell out of me, too! When I yelled to them to come back, they of course laughed and continued to run. I was shining my flashlight on the ground, and what did I see, but their clothes. You guessed it: I confiscated their clothes and yelled to them as they were running, "You can come to headquarters for your clothes!" Needless to say, the next night when I came into work, their clothes were still there. Knowing that the Great Swamp is not an ideal place to be on summer nights, I am sure they had some explaining to do when they finally arrived home.

As part of our nightly patrol duties, we would patrol through the Fairmount Country Club and check their maintenance garages. Often we would find keys in tractors or golf carts and confiscate them until the morning so no one would take them for joy rides. We also used to check the club's pool in the summer months for pool hoppers. Yes, sometimes the pool hoppers would leave their clothes on the fence, and we would take their clothes and remind them where they could retrieve them if they ran away.

Well! Aren't You Special.

The U.S. federal government only issues diplomatic plates for its own vehicles and vehicles owned by foreign diplomats. Until the eighties, diplomatic plates were issued by the state in which the consulate or embassy was located. Depending on their rank, top diplomatic officers have full immunity, as do their deputies and families. They cannot be arrested or forced to testify in court. We had a family in town who had diplomatic plates, and the officers were told that the husband was a diplomat with the United Nations in New York. The family had school-age children and was never involved in any police-related incidents as far as I know. I'm sure we all have pet peeves, and mine at one time was people parking their vehicles in emergency zones when there was other available parking nearby. One day in 1982 while on patrol in the Hickory Square Mall, I observed a vehicle parked for some time in the fire zone. The vehicle had diplomatic plates, and no one was around. This was around lunchtime. I radioed to my sergeant and told him the situation because I had never before ticketed a vehicle with diplomatic plates. The sergeant wasn't sure what to do, either, and told me to put a warning notice on the vehicle. While I was writing a warning, the driver and his family came out of a pizza parlor in the mall. The driver was adamant that he could not receive a summons due to his diplomat status. I explained that he was only getting a warning, and he grinned.

Only a few weeks later, the same vehicle was parked in a handicapped zone. I issued the appropriate summons and left. The patrol lieutenant called me into the office at the time, and he asked me what I was doing. I asked who this diplomat thought he was parking illegally and flaunting his diplomatic status. I said I would continue to write him summonses if he continued to park illegally. Someone in our police department made contact with the U.N., and apparently the diplomat was spoken to. We never had another problem with him. One small victory for common sense and fair play!

Pork Chop Hill

There was one particular apartment complex that some of us nicknamed Pork Chop Hill because it was the locale for some of the wildest and most challenging calls. During my second year on the force, I was working the midnight shift one evening with a sergeant on the desk and another officer with more seniority. The sergeant sent us to respond to a call in this apartment complex. He said a man was holding his wife hostage. It was the middle of the night, and as I was driving down the portion of Southern Boulevard known as Snake Hill, I had a flashing vision of life passing by me. I arrived on the scene, and about thirty seconds later my backup arrived. We approached the building and began alerting and evacuating other residents. While we were en route to the scene, more information had come in: the man in question had a shotgun to his wife's head and was threatening to kill her. There were no SWAT teams or ERT teams then; it was just my partner and I. I know the sergeant on the desk was wishing he were at the scene. Because we shared the radio frequency with neighboring communities New Providence and Chatham Borough, they heard the call and offered assistance if needed. We could always count on them.

My partner and I gained entry to the apartment with the help of the superintendent for the complex. While en route to such calls, all you can think about is planning your moves based on the information given by the dispatcher. Once at the scene, my partner and I went over a plan on how we would enter the bedroom. We decided that one of us would go high and the other would go low; we would both have weapons drawn, of course. We rushed though the bedroom door. Lying on the bed was the wife, and the husband did indeed have a shotgun. The shotgun was pointed at the door through which we had entered. We disarmed him without a shot being fired. The woman was safely removed from the apartment and stayed with a neighbor until we were finished. The husband, who was in his late fifties, was inebriated. He was arrested and transported to headquarters for processing. After processing, our judge was notified and bail was set. He was transported to the Morris County Correctional Facility in default of bail and to receive a psychiatric examination. As a result, it was discovered that along with having excessively consumed alcohol, the man had suffered a major mental breakdown. We were never called back to the residence.

When It's Time, It's Time

Thanks to my squad, a newborn baby girl arrived safely at Saint Barnabas Hospital in Livingston. It was mid-January 1991 around 4:40 p.m, which was when rush hour traffic was just picking up. Headquarters received a cell phone call from an OB/GYN physician on Fairmont Avenue stating that she was en route to St. Barnabas with a pregnant woman. Because the woman was experiencing complications, the doctor asked that they receive a police escort. Normally, police departments do not provide this service, but there are exceptions. An officer on my shift named Vinny located the vehicle by Sunset Terrace. The doctor informed the officer that the woman was eight months pregnant, and her contractions were two minutes apart. This quick-thinking officer knew there was no time to call our first aid squad, so he placed the pregnant woman in his patrol vehicle and asked the doctor to follow him. The other officers working this shift covered our intersections, and our dispatcher alerted all the other towns that we would be driving through and asked them to clear our route. I followed the car of the officer with the pregnant woman all the way to Saint Barnabas, where a team from the emergency room was waiting. It wasn't more than thirty seconds after our arrival that the woman gave birth to her baby daughter; we had made it just in time.

I returned back to town, and the other officer remained at the hospital until he knew that the mother and baby were all right. There had been great cooperation between our neighboring communities and great work from our dispatcher and officers. The only downside of this call was that the next day I was questioned why I had left town with the other officer to escort the women. I explained that had the other officer needed help, no one would be present to assist him, and time was of the essence. At the time I was a sergeant, and I had made the decision. There were no repercussions from my supervisors. This story is an example of both the many split second decisions an officer has to make and the reasons why superiors should not behave like Monday morning quarterbacks toward their officers. I have always believed that when you delegate a task to someone, you have to grant him or her decision-making authority.

The Night We Met Jesus

One of the many things that a police officer appreciates and values is a good partner or backup officer. It is rare to have a partner who, to some extent, can read your mind, but this type of person is invaluable. In this particular incident, Pete and I were working the 4:00 p.m. to 12:00 p.m. shift. To refresh your memory, the day book, which I mentioned in a previous story, was the book in which we wrote down alerts or things happening in town; we would read the incident logs from the previous day or two so that we would know what was happening. One residence off Fairmount Avenue housed a family with a daughter who had invited a male friend to live with them. This arrangement, in which four grown adults shared a residence, was a little crowded for the small Cape Cod-style home. For weeks, the male visitor had been acting strange. Though we all have our own definitions of strange, he was keeping weird hours, staying awake late into night, and frequently quoting scripture while walking around the house. If the parents were watching a show, he would turn off the television so that they could all pray. The family eventually decided that this man was no longer welcome in their home. The man also raised concerns with the neighbors regarding their children's safety. A few times people called the police department, and officers responded. But according to the officers who responded those times, there was no reason or probable cause to make an arrest.

On this particular day, Pete and I had just started our shift when were dispatched to this residence. When we arrived, we met the owners, who were in their middle-to-upper seventies and in visibly frail health. During our conversation with them, we learned that though they were fed up with his behavior, he refused to leave. They expressed their fear for both their own and their daughter's lives. Others in the neighborhood were also alarmed because this man had been observed walking up and down the street in what looked like a robe with a Bible in hand. After speaking with the parents and neighbors, Pete and I walked into the home and clearly identified ourselves even though we were in uniform. Immediately, this individual began ranting that he was Jesus Christ and was here to save the world; the world was full of sinners who would have to be punished. We also noticed that furniture had been thrown around; the owners claimed that he was the one responsible. As our conversation continued, he became boisterous and began preaching with animated hand gestures. He pushed me hard in my chest (an action that legally qualifies as assault) and ordered us to leave. I immediately placed him under arrest, and Pete handcuffed him. We transported him to headquarters. Our municipal judge was notified, and he set bail at $5,000. This man was subsequently transported to Morris County Jail and placed under psychiatric watch and care. Later we learned that he had been transported to a state psychiatric hospital. Weeks later, our department learned that the daughter who had been dating this individual had moved out of her parents' home.

Happy Saint Patrick's Day

One particular Saint Patrick's Day, one of the year's highest holy days for the Irish, was memorable. This night I witnessed an incident that I'd heard of but had never previously witnessed. Just after our shift began around 11:30 p.m., I was traveling westbound down Shunpike Road away from Lafayette Avenue and toward Noe Avenue. I suddenly saw headlights in my lane; the vehicle ahead was traveling eastbound in the westbound lane. I activated my overhead lights, but the car did not pull over onto his side of the road. I radioed in to headquarters because I had very little room on the road and was not able to pull over safely. The vehicle I was observing was not speeding but was in my lane of travel. As we got closer, the vehicle finally pulled over to the right side of the road. I turned my vehicle around and stopped him at the traffic light at the intersection of Shunpike Road and Lafayette Avenue. As I approached the driver, I could detect an odor of alcohol. Upon speaking with him and asking for his license, registration, and insurance card (a procedure just like the one you see on *Cops*), I could hear his slow and often slurred speech. His fumbling of the documents didn't help him, either. I had him exit the vehicle and perform a few sobriety tests. At that time the tests administered were mostly placing finger to nose, walking heel to toe, and reciting the alphabet. He failed these tests miserably.

This man had resided in Chatham Borough his whole life and was well known in the community. He was sixty-five years of age. I placed him under arrest and transported him to headquarters for processing, which included completing required paper work and having him submit to a Breathalyzer test. In our process room, we had a video camera that could record the DWI arrest as evidence that could be used in court or shown to the arrested person's attorney. Once inside the process room, this gentleman performed the same tests as the ones on the road, but this time he performed them better than most. He submitted to a Breathalyzer test and indicated that he wanted to prove a point to me that he wasn't drunk. He hadn't even realized that he had been driving on the wrong side of the road. He completed the Breathalyzer test with a .20 BAC reading, which was then double the legal limit. If ever there was a classic drunk driving case, it was this one. We transported this gentleman home after he had been processed and received his summons.

A few weeks later I was advised that he was pleading not guilty. Because our judge in Chatham Township was familiar with him, the case was transferred to Madison Borough. Such a transfer often happens when there might be a conflict of interest; it is admirable and ethical of the judges and lawyers to conduct themselves in this fashion.

Court night came about a month after the initial arrest. On the witness stand I swore to tell the truth, the whole truth, and nothing but the truth. Over the course of two consecutive nights, I spent five hours on the witness stand. Keep in mind that after court I had to work my regular shift from 12:00 a.m. to 8:00 a.m. DWI trials are mostly bench trials, which have only a judge who hears evidence and no jury. Evidence can include witness testimony and physical evidence like the videotapes from the arrest. The results of the case were shocking! The judge found the defendant not guilty based on the sobriety tests performed in front of the camera. Essentially, the judge didn't believe my testimony of the man's inability to perform sobriety tests on the road, and he ignored the scientific evidence taken from the Breathalyzer. Although members of the New Jersey State Police Breathalyzer Unit testified on the reliability of the machine, this judge didn't care. He seemed to base his decision solely on the testimony of the defendant and the video of the sobriety field tests conducted in headquarters. This drunk driving case was the only one I ever lost. Needless to say, I didn't need coffee that night to keep me awake for my midnight shift.

The next day after I woke up, I called Mothers Against Drunk Driving (MADD) and Students Against Drunk Driving (SADD) and told them about the case. They were as shocked as I was; even the New Jersey State Police Breathalyzer Unit in Trenton was in total disbelief. Beginning on the next court night and for several months afterward, MADD and SADD had representatives sit and observe this particular judge and how he handled drunk driving cases. A few months later I learned that the Borough of Madison had chosen not to renew his contract.

I remember another night well for an incident that doesn't happen very often. On the Green Village side of town, a well-planned drunk driving task force was set up on Loantaka Way. The task force was following the guidelines established by *Delaware v. Prouse* (1979). The court in this case determined that police could no longer randomly stop vehicles. Therefore, the officers had to make sure their sobriety checkpoint followed the rules as to how many vehicles could be stopped and how many personnel could be present. I had hoped to work the DWI post because the hours would have been overtime, and the federal government was paying the tab. If the original date had been kept, I also would have been able to work the detail with Pete. But the date was changed because not everyone would have had a chance to work the detail.

I was on stationary patrol by our old town hall building on the corner of Fairmount Avenue and Southern Boulevard (otherwise known as Snake Hill). Pete had the A side of town, I had the B side, and the sergeant was on the desk because we had no dispatcher that night. You might ask yourself, "What is stationary patrol?" The intersection at which I was sitting had a traffic light and two "No Turn on Red" signs. I was there to observe traffic for violators. A vehicle came up Southern Boulevard and turned right while the light was still red. I followed the vehicle a short distance, activated my overhead lights, and stopped the vehicle. By the time I had approached the driver's door, my backup had arrived and stopped on the other side of the car. I detected a strong odor of alcohol, and the driver fumbled for his credentials and had a disheveled appearance. I asked him to exit the vehicle so I could administer sobriety tests, which he failed. Pete already had the handcuffs out, and after we had cuffed the suspect, he identified himself as a prominent chef. He asked whether there was anything he could do to get out of the arrest. We replied no. He then said that he would service us and dropped to his knees. We placed him in the rear of my patrol car, transported him to headquarters, and processed him. He registered a .22 BAC reading on the Breathalyzer. The irony is that Pete and I made two DWI arrests that evening, and the DWI task force made none! A month or so later when the case was called, the driver pled guilty, received a fine, and lost his driver's license for two years.

House Fires

I remember two house fires very distinctly. One occurred while I was patrolling Deer Run Circle, and the other occurred on Buxton Road. While patrolling Deer Run Circle around 2:00 am, I observed flames inside a house. I radioed it in to the dispatcher, exited my vehicle, ran to the front door, and banged on it to wake the residents who were sleeping. The fire had started in their Christmas tree, which was near their fireplace, and quickly spread to the curtains, drapes, and furniture. You have to remember that the town had two excellent volunteer fire departments. Some of the officers responded to the scene while others went to the firehouse for fire apparatus. The Chatham Emergency Squad was also dispatched and provided excellent care to the family in the form of warm blankets and drinks until other arrangements could be made. Fortunately, this family of five as well as their dog survived.

While patrolling on another midnight shift, headquarters received a call of smoke in a house on Buxton Road. The sergeant and I were the only officers working the road that night. We both responded and simultaneously arrived at the scene. We literally carried two of the four residents out of the house. The other two residents ran out of the home. Later it was determined that the fire had started with an electric blanket, which had set the mattress on fire and created a heavy smoke condition. They were all transported to Overlook Hospital in Summit, treated for smoke inhalation, and released.

Food Network Had Nothing on Us

Most municipal, county, and city police departments in the United States operate on a twenty-four seven schedule 365 days of the year. This means that while most people are home on special occasions and holidays like Easter, Thanksgiving, and Christmas, police officers are working: patrolling, checking houses and businesses, answering medical assist and crime-in-progress calls, and performing the occasional welfare check. A welfare check happens whenever the police department receives a call from someone who has not heard from a relative for a period of time and cannot reach him or her by phone. Officers will respond to the residence and check on the person who lives there. Some obvious reasons are that the residents are out for the day or that the phone is either off the hook or out of order. The worst-case scenario is that the person has died and may have been dead for some time. As an officer I soon learned to keep a small jar of Vicks Vapor Rub in my briefcase just in case I received this type of call. I soon became keenly familiar with the odor that sometimes came from the residences where I performed welfare checks. In my career this outcome occurred a few times a year, especially with our older residents.

While working these holidays, we would often think of having a cookout ourselves, but one or more of us would always be on the road. Many police departments have areas or zones of patrol that assigned officers can't leave unless they are on a call or have asked permission to do so. So in order to have a cookout, we had to convince the sergeant on duty to allow all of us to come together and eat. After much coaxing, we were able to convince most of the sergeants to allow this meal. Of course, after some of them were promoted to a higher rank, they ceased to allow it. Sometimes we followed their rules, and other times we didn't. Some members of the administration often forgot what it was like to perform shift work. These cookouts usually occurred on the midnight shift, and in Chatham we could reach any point in town within three minutes with our vehicles' lights and sirens on. As Murphy's Law dictates, we would inevitably get a call for assistance just as we sat down to eat. The officers usually weren't thrilled about answering the call, but we had ground rules: if you got a call either on your side of town or in your area or zone, you had to respond. Rarely did we have cookouts on the dayshift; I can count on one hand how many times during my career we had them on the dayshift.

The invitation list for our cookouts eventually expanded to include other towns. We used to get together with officers from Harding Township, Madison, and Chatham Borough. It was almost like a potluck supper because everyone brought something. I used to bring meatballs and pasta that my wife had made earlier in the day. Someone else brought a salad, another brought Italian bread, and of course we had dessert. We didn't have these cookouts often, maybe once every other month, but when we did we had a good time. We always ended up talking about what was going on in our individual towns. The cookouts were about networking and sharing information, which really benefited both the communities and us. We shared criminal activities going on in our communities, and this sharing of information resulted in arrests. Certain times we sat at the picnic table outside the entrance to the police department, while in cold weather we brought the picnic table into the building. We always made sure to put it back before the day shift arrived.

Operation Reassurance

Operation Reassurance is a program that serves senior citizens who call seven days a week. The requirement is that the senior citizen calls the police department daily by 10:00 a.m.; if he or she does not, then a patrol vehicle is sent to his or her home. If the senior citizen is going away, he or she notifies the police department. Usually, a key is kept at police headquarters in a locked box, and officers have emergency contact information in the event they have to gain entry. Often, these calls were the most pleasant part of my shift. The people were always friendly and grateful that we were on the other end of the phone. One of the participants in the program worked on the Manhattan Project, a research and development undertaking during World War II that produced the first atomic weapons. Along with our other successful outreach programs for senior citizens, Operation Reassurance was a good community policing program.

One of our Operation Reassurance members had recently installed deadbolt locks on her front door. One evening when my squad was working, we received a call from this woman; she was unable to lock her front door. One of my officers responded. He was gone for some time, and I began to wonder what was taking him so long to complete this simple public assist call. Later I found out that he had replaced the lock altogether with a new one. The homeowner was not strong enough to fully lock her front door and didn't want to go to bed with it unlocked. The officer took it upon himself to replace her locks with another set of locks. This same officer a few months later was working the desk when an elderly female, also a participant in Operation Reassurance, called and mentioned that her doorbell had not worked in a long time. You guessed it: the same officer responded and fixed her doorbell, but this time he did it after working his twelve hour shift. I was very fortunate to work with such caring officers that particular year. We had a great squad!

Community Policing

The term community policing is of recent origin. I remember hearing stories about my paternal grandfather, who had been a police officer in Summit years ago. According to the stories he had a walking beat that included walking from River Road to the center of Summit. He checked businesses and residences and knew all the kids on his beat. Of course, kids then were outside playing sports or other games; they were not in the house playing video or computer games. When I was a manager for the A&P Tea Company, I once spoke with Mr. Joseph Twill, a Vice-President and General Manager of the Eastern Division of the A&P. He lived in Chatham Borough for many years. I introduced myself to Joe Twill one day in the Summit A&P. He remembered that my grandfather would always come into the A&P for a cup of Eight O'Clock coffee whenever he walking his beat. Mr. Twill also told me that my grandfather was very well-liked and respected. He was always polite and knew everyone on his beat; my grandfather was practicing real community policing long before the term itself came into our vocabulary.

As a new police officer, I was escorted around the first few days and introduced to various people in town. One of them was a guy named Harry, who used to own the Fairmount Deli located on Fairmount Avenue near Meyersville Road. I was fortunate to have met the Schwartz family who resided on Southern Boulevard. Many of our officers were very good friends with the Schwartz family, in fact, we used to call their home Post 99. The Schwartz family opened their home to the officers if they wanted to eat their lunch or dinner there.

I remember the race riots of the sixties. One of the programs that came from that era was the establishment of the Community Services Bureau or Community Relations Officers. The cops who were stuck in their ways thought that these programs were wastes of time. However, Police Athletic League (PAL), an offshoot of these programs, was quite popular. Community policing is a partnership between the police and their communities intended to solve the communities' problems. Fast forward to the late seventies and early eighties in Chatham Township. As our community grew in population, so did our crime, though not at a drastic rate. In 1979 and1980 our town experienced a high number of break-ins and forced entries. Residents had to be educated about not leaving their homes or vehicles unlocked. Money from the state and federal governments became available, and four officers from our department were sent to crime prevention school to become crime prevention practitioners. I was chosen to be one of those officers. We initiated neighborhood block watches, and neighborhood crime prevention signs were erected strategically throughout the community after specific compliance was established. Compliance means that at least 85 percent of the neighbors agree to be part of the community crime prevention efforts. Neighborhood block captains were named, and meetings were held often to update the communities. We frequently held these types of meetings at our schools and town hall. A business watch was formed as well.

One of our tactics that is still used in many municipalities has an officer park his or her patrol vehicle and walk the malls. We were fortunate that our town had only two malls and approximately sixty businesses total. Hassler's Pharmacy, Smith's Florist, Hickory Tree Deli, Wine Cellar,

Buxton's Ice Cream, and all the gas stations in town (to name a few) were very supportive of the police. Collectively, these business establishments helped preserve our small-town atmosphere. We looked out for each other, and we the police especially appreciated their civic-mindedness.

Our police department earned a reputation for stopping more vehicles than other police did in nearby towns. Primarily these vehicles were stopped for a legitimate reason and not for random checks. The word quickly spread to the bad guys that they ran a higher risk of getting stopped in our town compared to others. How did we know this? We interviewed jailed criminals and others who had been arrested and confessed that they should have gone to another town and stayed away from Chatham Township. One of the things I missed most when I became an administrator was not working with the public on a daily basis. There was not one business in town where I did not know most of the workers or with which I did not have a good relationship

Shifting

Police officers work all types of shifts and schedules. Shifts are different from schedules. Shifts can mean working 6:00 a.m. to 2:00 p.m., 7:00 a.m. to 3:00 p.m., or 8:00 a.m. to 4:00 p.m. The evening shifts usually begin at 3:00 or 4:00 p.m. and last until 11:00 p.m. or 12:00 a.m. The midnight shift was usually 11:00 p.m. to 7:00 a.m. or 12:00 a.m. to 8:00 a.m. There were years when we worked 7:30 a.m. to 3:30 p.m., 3:30 p.m. to 11:30 p.m., and 11:30 p.m. to 7:30 a.m. The half hour difference did make it easier for us commuters. I cannot understand why many of the officers who lived in town were never early for work; they usually arrived on the dot or a few minutes late. I was always and still am an early person, and when I was an officer, I expected to be relieved on time.

Things got better when I became a shift supervisor, or sergeant. It was much later in my career that we switched to twelve-hour shifts. The chief at the time asked me and a few other officers to research these shifts and see what we thought. We researched other towns that were working it, and they were mostly from northwestern Morris County.

After we presented our research to the chief, we heard rumblings from the lieutenants that they would never see the officers except when they worked day shifts, which were 7:00 a.m. to 7:00 p.m. However, the truth of it is that the officers weren't crazy about seeing the administration every day. Also, there were other duties, including court appearances, in-service training, and other types of department functions. I was one of three officers who did not want to switch from the eight-hour shift to the twelve-hour shift, but I was not going to stand in the way of progress. A compromise was reached between the chief and the PBA members in which we would try the new twelve-hour shift for ninety days. This ninety-day tryout period would give us plenty of time to see which kinks or challenges the new shift presented and how could we address them.

I remember going home one day and telling my wife and children that we were going to a new shift whose hours would be 7:00 a.m. to 7:00 p.m. and 7:00 p.m. to 7:00 a.m. One thing I remember telling them was that when I worked that that would be my sole focus, and afterwards I would have four days off. We also agreed to two-week shift schedules instead of switching every week. I had to admit that after working one full cycle of this new shift, the time off shift schedule was great. The old schedule gave us only a few full weekends off each year. The new one granted us seventeen partial and full weekends off. I was now able to coach my children's sporting activities or at least to watch them play without taking time off. It was also a bonus to enjoy a few days at our home in Vermont instead of needing to travel home after just one or two. The lieutenants were still not happy, but the new shift schedule eventually grew on them. After retiring from the police department, I earned my doctoral degree, and the topic of my dissertation was studying the effects of the eight-hour and twelve-hour shifts on officers with respect to their satisfaction, health, and social issues. In short, there were no significant differences between the eight-hour and twelve-hour shifts within the three areas of study.

Schedules were horrendous in the early days of my career (mid-seventies to late eighties). When I began my career, we worked five eight-hour shifts on and two days off, five eight-hour shifts on and two days off, five eight-hour shifts on and one day off. The town then owed us a day off every month. We were essentially working extra time and, instead of overtime pay, were given compensatory time off. As far as shifting went, we rotated from midnight shift to evening shift to day shift. It wasn't until later years that we switched to the four and four schedule, during which we worked two weeks of days and two weeks of nights. We had heard that the FBI had conducted extensive research on shift work along with the National Institute of Justice (NIJ). We contacted the FBI, and their research indicated that the longer you worked any one shift or schedule, the better you would perform. Therefore, their conclusion was that working a steady shift instead of rotating shifts was easier on your circadian rhythm because your body would have time to adjust.

The Promotional Process!

Because I participated in the promotional process for many years, I noticed that our department never promoted the same way twice. In New Jersey police officers can be promoted and move up in rank through three common methods: civil service, the New Jersey State Chiefs Association Test, or promotional policies devised by the town. Chatham Township is not a civil service community. Many towns promote strictly based on seniority, and officers will wait for a superior officer to retire or move on. Our department used to promote in that way, but right before I was hired, politics caused an officer to be skipped over for promotion. When I was hired the Chief of Police was Theodore Knispel, who was a very good chief who cared about his officers' community and department. He lived in town, was married, and all his children were wonderful. He passed away in 1978 after a short illness. The captain at the time was named acting chief of police, but he was ready to retire. He wanted to move out west to Arizona. There was a promotional test conducted by the township, and only the sergeants and two lieutenants were eligible to take the test.

As a result Detective Lieutenant George Conrads was named chief, and other promotions were made. After George became chief, the promotional process was changed again; the New Jersey State Chiefs of Police would administer it. This new process involved a grueling test, which consisted of written, oral, physical, and psychological portions. The test for sergeant was opened to all patrolmen including me. I was not ready because I had only been at the department for a few years, and I knew who the movers and shakers were. There were some officers who really deserved it, and then there were the officers who always showed up for the photo opportunities and were less deserving. We all know those types of people.

I remember studying for the sergeant's exam, for which we had to read about five different textbooks on police supervision, management, and criminal law. Along with answering questions on practical supervision scenarios, we also had to possess a familiarity with our township ordinances and our community. On the day of the exam, I wore a suit and tie. When I walked into the conference room, I noticed three chiefs of police in uniform standing about twenty-five feet away from me. I relaxed because I knew I wasn't going to make it, but I still wanted to do well. There was an hour-long interview and some quizzing on current case law (in which they always threw in some obscure terms and laws). When the process had finished, I, like everyone else who had undergone the ordeal, began second-guessing myself. I wondered what I could have done better, how I would work with these new sergeants, and whether there be any animosity if I were one of the officers selected. Our department was in what I called the adolescent stage; we were growing, and both the town and the demand for services were growing. More stores were being added to the malls, and low- and moderate-income housing was coming, a development that didn't make many of the old-time residents happy. Other tracts of land were also being developed throughout the township. The old "not in my neighborhood" syndrome was very apparent. It was okay for these folks to live elsewhere, but they could not live here with us.

Within a few years, we had a manual of rules and regulations. I don't think NYPD created as many rules as they wanted to, but we were able to read them over, and our local union (the NJ State Policemen's Benevolent Association or PBA) was able to negotiate the regulations that really treated the officers unfairly. I was the PBA delegate for sixteen years before I was promoted to the rank of sergeant in 1990.

After a year or so, another sergeant's test was announced, and a new policy regarding the system was put in place. The written portion of the test now had fewer percentage points than the oral board and in-house evaluation. I knew this would be the test that would promote me—or so I thought. My chances were better because the test would create two new sergeants. All the applicants went through the same stressful preparations for ninety days. We wanted to succeed, so we studied constantly and chose not participate in family functions. When the results came out, I learned that I had placed third. Someone with fewer years' experience than I had would be promoted, as would someone with a lot of seniority. It was ironic that one of the new sergeants had one year of experience twenty times over yet had enrolled in County College of Morris just before the test had been announced. Why? So that when he went into the oral board with the chiefs he would be able to say that he was enrolled in college. To my knowledge, he never continued with the college courses.

In the period in between tests, I served in the traffic safety unit, administration, and flex unit (which included two weeks in the detective bureau and two weeks on the road). A few years later, Chief Robert Scherer, who had given me an opportunity in the detective bureau, appointed me to detective, and I loved every minute of it. In the detective bureau, you were always busy, and I worked on some interesting cases. After the town's first bank robbery, I was able to investigate and work with the FBI and state police, and eventually our leads led to an arrest months later. I give Bob Scherer a lot of credit; some officers used to say that he was not an easy person to work for, but he was a straight shooter, and I work well with someone like that. He did not micromanage the people he trusted.

I eventually took another sergeant's test, and I ranked number one. The promotion, though, was held up for nine months because of a lawsuit brought by another officer against the town. I won't go into the details, but the suit was directed at the promotional process and not at me personally. The town eventually won the case, and I was promoted to the rank of sergeant on August 2, 1990. Chief Scherer retired a year or so later, and then Captain Thomas Ramsey was promoted to chief. He, too, eventually retired. At this point, the department and town were really going through some growing pains. We went from a department of twelve officers in 1976 to a department of thirty-two officers at our peak in the mid- to late-nineties.

The promotion process changed yet again, and this time I was eligible to test for chief of police. I had no interest in being the chief of police, but I knew from experience that if I took this test, I might receive another promotion like captain or lieutenant. The new test for the chief's position consisted of an oral interview with the town council and an evaluation at an assessment center. I was probably more relaxed for this interview than for any other I've ever had. I remember walking out of the hour-long interview and thanking God for allowing me to remember things; it almost felt as though he had been putting words in my mouth. I felt great! Later, I was told I was moving on to the assessment center. Five of us were at the assessment center for the test, which was an in-basket test. We were given scenarios for which we had to develop strategies, plans, and methods with which to execute those plans. We were videotaped so the testers could observe, among other things, how we worked with others and who was assertive and who was more passive. As a result of the testing, George Kurzenknabe was named chief of police, and I was promoted to the rank of lieutenant. I heard from a few town hall employees with whom I enjoyed a great relationship that another administrator had been working behind the scenes to have them promoted to a higher rank than I had received. The move this person had been planning, though, did not happen. I thoroughly enjoyed being lieutenant and running the patrol division, which was the largest unit in the department. This division included all the patrol officers and sergeants, training, the Office of Emergency Management (OEM), scheduling, payroll, overtime assignments, special assignments from the chief, and other assigned duties. It was a rank I enjoyed until I retired. The other lieutenant was in charge of the two-member detective bureau and other assigned duties. Chiefs Scherer and Kurzenknabe were the best chiefs of police I ever worked for, and I would work for them again in a heartbeat.

Riding with Partners

Depending on the size of the police department, most small to mid-size police agencies have officers who ride alone in their patrol vehicles. Every now and then, the officers have to double up or ride with another officer in the patrol vehicle. When I was an officer, we normally rode by ourselves. I had my share of partners, but one in particular should have been retested several times for his driver's license. Someone actually could have suffered whiplash from the way he drove. Gas, brake, gas, brake. Windows up, windows down, heat on, heat off, air conditioning on, air conditioning off—he was a little obsessive-compulsive. He was a good officer in his day, but the job was changing, and you had to know when to leave. I enjoyed riding with a more senior officer when I was new to the force, but the arrangement grew old after a while, and I wanted to be on my own. Some of the officers also smoked, and the smoking bothered me.

Domestic Violence

It wasn't until I was in the administration that I realized how many domestic violence and abuse calls our officers responded to in a year. I know in my career I had to respond to too many. In one year alone in our township of 8,500 people, we responded to thirty-five domestic violence calls that resulted in one of the spouses or partners being removed from the home. During my tenure as a police officer, I saw a marked change over the years in how domestic violence cases were handled. Officers used to just separate the two parties for the night and warn them not to let this situation happen again. Eventually, though, even the slightest mention of pain meant someone had to be arrested. In the police department we have made a 180-degree turn in favor of the victim. Officers have to make tough calls during domestic violence incidents. The mandatory arrest policy is a good one and should have been implemented years ago. The definition of who could be a victim was also expanded. At one time, men and partners living together were not considered covered by the domestic violence act; now they are.

I remember one 11:00 p.m. call on Susan Drive. A woman called and said that her husband was going to hit her, and she needed help. I responded with another officer, and both the husband and the wife greeted us. They were standing apart from one another, and when we asked what the problem was, they told us what had really happened. The wife had purchased a $5,000 rug for their dining room even though she knew that her husband was going to lose his job. She didn't deny it; she just said that she had wanted the rug. We could tell that they were both intoxicated, and there were no signs of physical injury. The wife had been more afraid that her husband would hit her after he found out about the rug. The husband agreed to stay at his parents' house in a neighboring town for the night.

I experienced another full-blown domestic violence fight just off Green Village Road. I was still fairly new to the police department when the dispatcher sent me to an address at which the caller had reported that her husband was throwing furniture around. While I was waiting for my backup, I could see through the window that this problem was escalating. There was no time to wait for my backup, who was coming from the other side of town. I entered the home; the husband was holding his wife by her hair and choking her. I subdued him and placed him in handcuffs, whereupon the wife jumped on me and began cursing me for arresting him. My backup arrived, and both were arrested on assault charges. Later in court, the wife dismissed the charges against her husband. She was simply found guilty of having assaulted me. You can't make this up!

Working holidays was never my idea of fun, but I knew that that was part of the job; on a police force, someone always has to work. I remember this one Thanksgiving Eve like it was yesterday. I was dispatched to a residence on Rose Terrace where a domestic dispute was occurring between a husband and wife. I was the only officer available because the others were on a call for accident investigation and medical aid. After I introduced myself, the husband and wife informed me that they were not married; they were divorced but living together. I asked, what seems to be the problem? The problem was that the ex-wife had refused to wash his socks; she had said that she was done with that chore. I looked at them both and said, "Really? This is what you called the police for—socks?" The wife said that the washer and dryer were on her side of the house, but she would not wash any of his things anymore. They were both heavily intoxicated, and they thought their divorce wasn't legal anymore; they thought that because they were living together, they were still married. So, remembering an episode of *NYPD Blue*, I had them place their right hands on my badge, and I declared them still divorced. They both thanked me, and we never got called back.

Nighttime Visitor

Before officers start their shifts, they usually read the day book I mentioned earlier and catch up with the reports compiled while they were off duty. I remember at the start of one shift I read a report about a husband and wife on Falmouth Road. This domestic call resulted in the husband's removal from the house with a restraining order of no-contact. I wrote the plate number down, and during my patrol I spotted the vehicle at the house. I radioed that I was at the residence and would check on the welfare of the resident. The wife answered the door with a drink in her hand and told me that she was okay. I asked if her husband was there, and she said yes. He then entered the door with a drink in his hand and smiled. She stated that she had been lonely and had missed her husband. I placed them both under arrest for violating the restraining order. They sat in the county jail from Friday night until Monday morning when a superior court judge was able to hear the case. You don't violate a restraining order because you're lonely. Think of the time and money that were involved in obtaining the restraining order. That behavior is a clear abuse of the system that was designed to protect victims of domestic abuse.

CSI Effects

Most of the burglaries in our town occurred during the day when the homeowners were away at work or on vacation. One particular burglary occurred while I was working. A resident of Ramapo Trail came home during the day because she had not been feeling well. She parked her vehicle in the driveway, and while walking to the garage door to enter her home, she observed a large amount of blood on the door, doorknob, and glass panes surrounding the door. The homeowner ran to a neighbor's house and called the police. When we responded, we found even more blood and a lot of shattered glass on the ground. We searched the house for a suspect or suspects. Eventually, the house was cleared, and nothing appeared to have been taken from the home. We initiated a neighborhood canvas that resulted in negative results, which meant that no one had seen a suspicious individual.

At the time we were conducting our canvas, Overlook Hospital Emergency Room was calling neighboring police departments to report that they were treating a male in his twenties for severe lacerations to his right arm. I responded to Overlook Hospital, and after questioning this individual, I determined that he had been responsible for the break-in. After he was treated for his lacerations, he was released into my custody. On the way to the police station, he confessed to having broken into the residence. He was not from our area and had randomly chosen the house in Chatham Township because it was right off Fairmount Ave. He thought he would have an easy time getting in and out.

The man was charged with burglary and was later indicted by the grand jury. A criminal history check revealed that he had priors for burglary and theft. He pled guilty before trial; he really had no other choice. At the time of the investigation, the Morris County Sheriff's Crime Scene Office had been notified and had responded to the scene to preserve and collect evidence. Had the defendant not pleaded guilty, then the blood collected at the scene would have matched his and would have served as evidence in court; this evidence would have ensured a guilty verdict.

Medical Emergencies

During my childhood and teenage years, I always thought that when you needed medical help at home, an ambulance would arrive and treat you, or it would transport you to the hospital. When I was five years old on the beach in Keansburg, my father fell into a hole left by kids playing in the sand. The ambulance came and transported him to Overlook in Summit, a long way from Keansburg. One of the first things a police officer does in our department is check that his vehicle is equipped with good working equipment, which can include oxygen, fire extinguishers, a halogen tool, gloves, rope, traffic cones, traffic vests, and a first aid kit. Not all police departments in New Jersey respond to medical aid calls. I didn't know this fact until after speaking with other officers from different communities. As an example, in some communities in Union County, the first aid squad will be dispatched for medical aid calls but not the police officers unless the situation is life-threatening. These are not the only towns that have this policy. Many communities have their own volunteer or paid first responders, and a few communities such as Union have paid firefighters on the ambulance (which is very comforting to know).

We are all on this earth for a certain amount of time, and we never know in advance when our time is up. I also believe that no matter what you do, when it's your time, it's your time. When our Lord turns the page and your name is on it for that day, it is your time to go home to God. In Chatham Township, the police officers are the first responders on a medical aid call, which can range in severity from a child falling off a bicycle to a person having a massive heart attack. As police officers we are the first to respond; we have to keep everyone calm and render basic first aid until a competent medical authority arrives to take over the patient's care. One type of call that always used to amaze me was whenever we would have to treat someone who had fallen into a diabetic coma. Most of the time, the patient was unconscious, and the family members were frantic. In our first aid kits we carried a glucose gel that we could apply to our fingers (after first putting on gloves) and swipe inside their gums. The gel looked like a tube of toothpaste but contained a highly concentrated level of sugar. You couldn't simply give this person a candy bar or orange juice; he or she was unconscious. If someone was still alert and his or her blood sugar was low, then the orange juice, candy bar, or other sweet treat could have worked. The first time I treated someone with this condition, I thought for sure the person had passed away. But within seconds—and I means seconds—of my administering the gel, the patient was alert and at first combative. Why combative? They were disoriented for a few minutes and then regained their composure. The cause was usually because they had eaten poorly that day or had forgotten to properly take their medicine. This type of call generally turned out well for everyone, and the family and friends loved us. But there were times when the patient had been left unattended too long, and there was nothing we could do except have them transported as soon as possible to a nearby hospital.

Recognizing the signs of a heart attack is important as well. We had our share of heart attack calls. I remember responding to a residence on Shunpike Road near the power lines. I knew the family members who lived there, and one day a call came in that their mother was not feeling well and was having severe back pain. I responded first, administered oxygen, and took vital signs (blood pressure and respiration levels) until the first aid squad could arrive. I was sitting on the couch with the woman, whom I had known for years, when she suddenly said that the back pain had subsided and that she would no longer go to the hospital. Despite her family members' urging her to go, she did not. Not a minute had passed before she turned to me on the couch and said, "Oh, my lower back really hurts all of a sudden." Unfortunately, those were her last words. CPR began immediately, and Medic I from Overlook Hospital responded; they provided advance life support (ALS). After exhaustive efforts, she passed away. This was a truly sad day, and my heart ached for them.

I also had a fair share of choking calls during my career. We would hear from the King James Nursing Home and also from several restaurants in town. One of the well-known restaurants was Buxton's (now out of business), which was in the corner of the Hickory Square Mall. We also had the 50-Yard Line, which was first the Hickory Tree

Inn and is now Charlie Brown's. The décor for the 50-Yard Line included a lot of football memorabilia and Giants jerseys hanging on the wall. The 50-Yard Line was known in the neighboring college communities as an easy place for underage patrons to be served. We responded to quite a few calls there for someone choking on dinner. There was nothing quite like running into one of these crowded places, finding the person choking, and hoping that you could save the individual with everyone watching you. I am happy to say that all the choking calls that I was on turned out all right for the patient. I remember a few times the manager of the 50-Yard Line asked me if I had to park in front of the door. So let's see…they had called us to help a choking patron and then wanted me to park where? No! My patrol car was staying put until I could clear the call and the ambulance, if needed, had arrived.

There was one choking call that didn't turn out all right. I was dispatched to the Chatham Hill Apartments off Southern Boulevard (Hickory Place) for a woman who was choking. I remember the husband indicated that he and his wife had just returned home from a day of shopping. She was in her mid-forties. I was a patrolman then, and I remember my sergeant also had responded to this call. After we entered the apartment, her husband told us that they had had pizza delivered. She had started to eat and begun to choke. It turned out that the cheese on the pizza had been very hot and had stuck to the woman's mouth and covered her throat. We feverishly exhausted every possible means by which we could save her. The first aid squad tried valiantly as well. She was transported to the hospital and later pronounced dead on arrival.

Drugs and Guns

One of my duties as a detective was to conduct drug investigations. In the early nineties I had developed an informant who was purchasing drugs from a local establishment where alcohol beverages were also sold. Knowing our department's limited manpower, I contacted the Morris County Prosecutor's Office and worked with its drug unit. The MCPO had the resources and manpower to assist with this investigation, especially after we determined that it was a more elaborate enterprise than it had first appeared. Several months passed, and we conducted a few controlled "buys." The investigation led us to a group of drug dealers from northern Morris County who would frequent this establishment and sell small amounts of marijuana and cocaine to people from the area. Affidavits were sworn to a county superior judge for the purpose of attaining search warrants. Our search warrant was executed on a Friday night at a location where we knew most of the participants would be present. In the end, eight individuals were charged with various drug offenses, depending on the quantity in their possession and their intent to distribute a controlled dangerous substance (CDS). It was a successful and gratifying end to a lengthy and complex investigation.

Hiring New Police Officers

I mentioned earlier I was promoted to the rank of sergeant in August 1990. Not long afterwards I was transferred from the patrol division to administrative sergeant. It was a lateral move, and one of its benefits included no shift work (working nights or midnights). My regular hours became 7:30 am to 3:30 pm, but of course, I had to be flexible. New responsibilities accompanied this rank: payroll, overtime, hiring and training crossing guards, overseeing emergency management, preparing press releases, acting as the PIO (public information officer), researching and planning, and pretty much anything else the chief or administration needed accomplished. I had to work with outside contractors who needed to hire off-duty officers for traffic control while they conducted construction roadwork. If a special event—like a carnival, car show, or the LPGA tournament—were going to occur in town, the administrative sergeant would attend the pre-event meetings and prepare SOPs (standard operating procedures) for the officers. The administrative sergeant reported directly to the chief of police.

Not long into this position, I was asked to be part of the interview process for new police officers. I remained on the interview board even after I had been promoted to the rank of lieutenant. The Chatham Township Police Department had received approval to hire two officers because two of our current officers had indicated that they intended to retire. The police and fire pension plan allowed officers to retire either with twenty years of service, twenty-five years of service, or the maximum number of thirty years of service. Most of the officers retired after twenty-five years of service. If an officer had been disabled for some reason, he or she could retire on disability as well.

Our police department advertised in our local paper, which was the *Chatham Courier,* along with the Morris County *Daily Record* and the *Star-Ledger.* Three to four weeks' notice was given for potential candidates to apply if they were interested. Along with the standard requirements of being a police officer, our department wanted to hire officers with a bachelor's degree. An applicant pool was established after some applicants were discovered to have had their driver's licenses revoked or suspended. (How can you be a police officer and drive a patrol vehicle without a license? You can't!) A few had careless driving citations, and one applicant had a DWI (driving while intoxicated) charge, which meant he could not drive for at least two years (we were not going to wait for him). After the applicants had passed the first phase, we administered the oral interviews. The chief and lieutenant usually conducted the oral interviews, and the administrative sergeant was involved in a few interviews. All members of the interview team had questions to ask the applicants, and of course we always asked whether the applicants had any questions for us. I almost couldn't believe some of the questions: "Do I have to work nights? My girlfriend prefers me to be home and sleep with her." "Do I get the holidays off? Because I usually stay with my family on the major holidays." "What type of car do I drive? Is it new?" "Do I get vacation this year?" I would bet that most of the police officers reading this book asked only one question: "When can I start?"

Can you imagine being asked these questions? After being asked the one about the holidays a few times, I started to respond, "Who do you think will be working the holidays? It won't be me!" Yes, police officers work twenty-four seven, 365 days a year. We don't turn off the lights at 11:00 p.m. and go home. These really were serious questions from some of the applicants. None of them were hired! You always could tell the applicants who were really hungry for the job. They displayed a passion to help people and to make the world a better place. They were hired. It is a major investment by a community when a police officer is hired. We are not hiring people to work at fast food chains who may last a year or two. Being a police officer is a profession, not a job.

Town Hall and Public Works

I mentioned earlier that when I went for my first interview to become a police officer, I had to report to the town hall. At that time the town hall was the old little red schoolhouse on the corner of Fairmount Avenue and Southern Boulevard. This little town hall building was also the location of our court two nights a month; it was also the site of many townships meetings like those for the planning or zoning boards. The personnel at our town hall were the nicest people you would ever want to meet. I remember meeting Alice Lundt, who was our town clerk and later our town administrator. Alice was incredibly bright and very resourceful. She was able to secure funding for a new town hall, which required the renovation of the former Mountainview School on Meyersveille Road so that all the town officers could be housed in one location. There was even talk about the police department moving from its location to Meyersville Road. Feasibility studies were conducted and included estimated response times from this potential headquarters to the farthest corners of our town. It turned out that it simply would take too long for our patrol officers to respond if we moved to Meyersville Road. I always found Alice to be a fair, compassionate, and nice person both socially and professionally. We also had our share of judges and court clerks, and most of us always worked well with them.

Our public works garage and offices were located behind our police department building on Southern Boulevard. Over the years, I watched them grow from a handful of workers to almost thirty in number. There was also a sewer plant operation off of Tanglewood Lane. Patrol vehicles operate twenty-four seven, 365 days a year. Ford seemed to win the bid for vehicle contracts year after year, but there were a few years when Dodge and Chevy won the bid. Not that I'm biased because of my name, but the Fords lasted longer and held up better than the other makes. There was a superintendent of public works and two road supervisors along with the other workers. Some were mechanics, and most worked on township-owned roads, performed other repairs, and maintained the parks in the township. Our vehicles had to have weekly maintenance checks, and we used to hope the workers would wash the cars. However, they did not, so some of our officers used to wash their own patrol vehicles. Public works personnel also installed our radio communication systems and emergency lights in our patrol cars. I enjoyed working with public works on many events.

Got Milk?

We have all seen and can relate to some of the commercials about running out of milk at the most inappropriate time. Our son Tim was born four weeks early in October of 1983 and required to be hospitalized for a longer period. At home was Tim's older brother and sister. My wife and I often took turns going to the hospital to visit and bottle feed him. This one Sunday evening, my wife handed me a bottle of mother's milk to bring to the hospital after my shift. At that time, I was working 8-hour shifts. I remember this night very well, it was a Sunday night and it was midnight to 8 am shift which also meant all the stores would be closed. When I arrived at work, I placed the bottle in the refrigerator, which was in a thermal type bag. The sergeant who was working the desk at the time whom we will call Bob, said to me, see if you can find some place open for milk so we could have it with our coffee. We were not allowed to leave town which would have been easier, especially since Madison and Summit had 24 hour convenience stores. I radioed in to headquarters that nothing was open. I thought to myself, I guess we'll be drinking coffee black tonight. At 1 or 1:30 am was my time for a coffee break and read reports from the previous shifts. I walked into the command desk where the sergeant was sitting drinking coffee. I looked over and saw it looked like it had milk in it. I said to him, where did you get the milk for your coffee? He replied, oh, someone left milk in a bottle in the refrigerator. I said, that is mother's milk for my son Tim! Oh………..He said! Got Milk?

Another Snowstorm?

Along with not liking to work the midnight shift, I had other dislikes. These included wearing boots. I dreaded snowstorms, and in the eighties and nineties we had plenty of snowstorms. Six years after being promoted to Sergeant, we had the Blizzard of '96. Over two feet of snow fell in early January. Schools closed for four to five days in some communities. New Jersey State Police drove legislators to Trenton so they could work. Not only for that week but also for many weeks afterward, I had to wear boots.

I remember other things about that winter. My squad of officers at the time consisted of three patrol officers, a dispatcher, and myself. That year, we worked sixteen snowstorms—yes, sixteen! We should have had shirts made up that said, "We survived all the snowstorms." Public works was also responsible for clearing the police department's walkway and driveways, and radio cars had to be moved around the lot for effective plowing. I previously mentioned that I got along well with the public works personnel. While my squad was working all these snowstorms, the same public works personnel were working them, too. We got along so well that they used to snow blow a path for us to get to our patrol vehicles safely. Not too many other squads had that service.

It was anything but fun and games when you had that much snow in a short period of time. We had several medical aid and fire calls, and we still had to respond to them regardless of the snow. You couldn't say, "It's snowing too hard, so we can't come to help you." One of our officers responded to a cancer patient on Meyersville Road, and the officer got physically stuck in a waist-deep snow bank. He tried climbing over the bank at the edge of the road while carrying our bulky first aid kit and an oxygen tank (an old version rather than the newer portable ones). A neighbor saw the officer sink into the snow bank, and he handed him a shovel and helped pull him out. Another resident was driving by with a Jeep Wrangler, pulled up with a plow, and plowed the bank so the officer could get to the house. The first responders arrived, and together they and the officer were able to get the resident to the hospital for treatment. A few of the officers could not get home at the end of their shifts and actually slept in the weight room at headquarters.

One of the many things that made me happy when I retired was not working in snowstorms. Instead, I could sit home either here in New Jersey or in Vermont in front of the fireplace.

Women in Law Enforcement

There were very few women in the law enforcement profession in the fifties and sixties. It was not until the late seventies and eighties that more women entered the law enforcement field. Many police departments, of course, had hired female special police officers to assist with matron duties. Matrons were used to frisk and search female prisoners. These specials were well-trained, but this position was usually part-time. Our department hired its first female officer in the mid-eighties. Fran was hired as a police officer from another community, and because she had already been trained, there was no need for the town to send her to the police academy. Even so, she had to learn our streets, businesses, and local ordinances, and she needed to familiarize herself with the culture of Chatham Township. As every police officer soon realizes, each town or municipality has its own identity.

Predictably, there was the usual grumbling from some people in town about a woman on the police force; but a majority of citizens supported it. Fran was an assertive and proactive police officer, and she had a good career in the police department. I had the opportunity to work with her on a few occasions, and then one year, she was assigned to my squad. We had a great year with many arrests and positive community relation efforts, and there was good camaraderie on our squad. Fran performed all the same duties as her male counterparts.

Another female officer was hired a few years later. Sharon had been a police dispatcher and a special officer. She was also very familiar with Chatham and the surrounding geographical area. Sharon was also a good officer. I especially remember one call that we were on together. This particular night shift, she had been patrolling along Southern Boulevard and had stopped a vehicle for suspected DWI. I heard the radio transmission and headed over to back her up, as is customary when only a few officers are working. Remember, we ride alone in the patrol vehicles. I remember hearing Sharon say over the radio that the driver was refusing to exit his vehicle. I was about a minute away when I heard this. When I arrived at the scene, Sharon had already gotten the driver out of the vehicle, handcuffed him, and placed him in the back seat of her patrol vehicle. Sharon later told me about her interaction with the driver. The driver had asked, "What are you stopping me for, Missy?" Sharon had asked for his driver's license, registration, and insurance card. He had refused to comply, and when asked to step out of his vehicle, he had replied, "No, make me." So she had pulled the driver out through the driver's window and promptly placed him under arrest. Later at headquarters, sobriety tests and a Breathalyzer test were administered. The Breathalyzer reading was double the legal limit. He was charged with DUI and released to the custody of someone who could drive. Later in the month, he appeared in court and pleaded guilty.

Today, more and more police departments are recognizing the value of having female police officers. I mentioned earlier that during my last year as a police officer, I began teaching criminal justice as an adjunct at the College of Saint Elizabeth. It was ironic that the very first course I had to teach was titled "Women in the Criminal Justice System." I was certainly well-prepared. It was unusual for a police department our size to have two female officers.

Yet these women certainly were qualified and had successful careers. I am grateful to them for helping me to realize the valuable contributions that women make to modern police work.

Play Nice with Others

As I mentioned earlier, when I first became a member of the police department, the patrol lieutenant drove me around town and introduced me to many residents and business owners. These included members of the Chatham Emergency Squad (which covered Chatham Borough and Chatham Township), the Green Village Fire Department, and the Long Hill Fire Department (later named the Chatham Township Fire Department). The first aid squad and fire departments were both only staffed by volunteers. No one was receiving a salary. Remember the story I mentioned earlier about the horse running at large? Well, the first person I had come into contact with during that case had been the Green Village Fire Chief, who happened to live on Green Village Road. He probably could discern from the look on my face that this had been my first horse running at large call.

All the volunteer agencies had personnel who were very well-trained, personable, and empathetic to the residents when called for their service. Imagine yourself sleeping in your nice, warm, cozy bed while the temperature outside is in the teens and snow is falling. Your beeper or pager goes off at 2:30 a.m., and you have to respond to a two-car accident with injuries and possible fuel spill. The part of the town in which the incident had occurred determined which fire department was going to respond. As for the first aid squad members, it didn't really matter where the call came from because they responded from where they lived, in either the borough or township. The fire department members responded to the firehouse to board their trucks with other firefighters. Some of the first aid squad members responded to the scene while others responded to their headquarters to bring the ambulance. As police officers, we were the first ones to arrive on the scene, and I for one was always glad to see first aid squad members arrive. We all knew our duties and worked well as a team. Often, after a more difficult call, we would meet back at the first aid squad station or the firehouse to discuss the call and assess how we all could have handled it differently.

Were there ever disagreements? Absolutely! A couple police officers I worked with could not put aside their egos; neither could some of the other first responders. However, this was the exception and not the rule. The main thing was that the patient or victim always came first! During my career, the police department had numerous training events with the first aid squad. It was very interesting to learn about the BLS (basic life support) procedures. I was inspired by many of the first aid members, and in 1979 I enrolled in an EMT (emergency medical technician) course. I also was a charter member of Overlook Hospital's Medic I Unit. Medic I was a mobile unit that responded to life-threatening calls. On board were a doctor, a nurse, and a driver. The drivers such as myself were usually police officers who had been trained in evasive driving (a very valuable course). The doctor and nurse were usually on duty in the emergency room at Overlook. We were stationed in an old house next to Overlook Hospital. When a call came in, we responded with lights and siren and often received police escorts to the scene because many of us were not familiar with the various communities we served. We responded mostly to heart attacks, strokes, and severe motor vehicle accidents. I volunteered for that unit for five years, and when I left the unit drivers finally began receiving pay. The medical training that I received prepared me to serve residents and family members in a more professional and knowledgeable manner. When my wife was pregnant with our children, I always volunteered to boil the water. My wife told me there was no way I was going to deliver our children. What can I say? I tried.

Camaraderie: Police Culture

Many of the books I read about police officers or the police force explore both their culture and the camaraderie among the blue (law enforcement officers). It is true that once you're a cop, you're always a cop. One might enter this profession with the assumption that everyone who needs help or wants help will welcome you warmly. That is not always the case. Some of my best friends (whom I still have today) worked on other police departments. Before I was promoted to the rank of Sergeant and was still serving as the PBA delegate, I met some wonderful officers from other towns at conventions; my wife and I socialized with them and their families. I had good friends on all the departments that surrounded Chatham Township: Summit, New Providence, Berkeley Heights, Long Hill Township, Harding Township, Morris Township, Madison, Florham Park, Mountain Lakes, and Chatham Borough. My best friends in whom I could confide anything even worked as far away as the Orange County Sheriff's Department in Orlando, Florida.

Due to the nature of the work that police officers perform, police officers usually never let their guards down. Earning a police officer's trust is not easy to do. Yet a strong camaraderie develops among officers when they are in the so-called "trenches" and answering the same types of calls. Some of the incidents or calls turn out all right, but some do not. It's tough working a child abuse case or a sexual assault case, and you need someone to talk to about such difficult matters. You cannot simply go home and talk to your wife or children about them. You have to remember that my midnight shift ended at 7:00 a.m. or 7:30 a.m. As I was walking through the door, my wife and children were going out the door to either work or school. Or if I finished my shift at midnight and arrived home at 12:30 a.m, I wasn't about to wake my wife and tell her about my shift. When my family reads this book, they will know more than what I used to tell them at home.

After handling a tough call, many of us would go out after our shift for something to eat and drink, and we would discuss that particular case and assess how we could have handled it better. Today, there are critical incident stress debriefing (CISD) teams and "Cop2Cop" programs where officers can go for assistance. Not many of these resources existed until the late 1990s. They can be quite helpful, but the next day officers are back at work ready to do it all again. There is a strong bond among law enforcement officers, first responders, fire personnel, and the nurses. Let's be honest: almost everyone loves firefighters, but not many people call the police to say, "Hey, we are having cake and coffee tonight. Would you like to stop by?" There were many houses in town, though, where I could always stop to enjoy a meal and friendship. I do think some of my friends were a little jealous, but they had the same opportunities that I did. In fact, many of them developed solid relationships in which I was not involved.

Today I still find myself looking at license plates, the colors of vehicles, and the ways they are being driven. I do not know why; after all, I cannot stop them anymore or radio in a complaint. When our family goes out for dinner, I still sit with my back to the wall and am always scanning the room. When we go to the mall, I'm always looking around for suspicious people or activity. I remember one time in the hardware section of the Sears Department Store, I observed a young male place a socket wrench set in his pants. I told the plainclothes officer working at the time, and he apprehended the male with the set still in his pocket. You are really never off duty, and that's what I mean when I say, "Once a cop, always a cop."

Cops usually socialize with other cops, as is the case with many people who share a profession. I remember going to a Christmas party with my wife at someone's home in Scotch Plains; I had not been enthusiastic about going but had gone anyway. Well, most of the teachers with whom my wife taught knew I was a police officer. I sat down, and one teacher came over and sat next to me. She said, "You know, I have a friend who got a speeding ticket…" And there went the night. Instead of a pleasant conversation about the weather, her children, or current topics, she had brought up her friend with the speeding ticket. No matter what I said to this woman, it was not going to satisfy her. As it turned out, she was the one who had gotten the ticket. I did not attend any more holiday parties that season or in subsequent years.

First Bank Robbery

Chatham Township experienced its first bank robbery in August 1989. I remember it well because I was a detective at the time. Our dispatcher called me a little after 9:00 a.m. and stated that the Chatham Savings and Loan in the Chatham Mall had just been robbed. I responded to the scene along with patrol officers, who had arrived first and already secured the scene. Thankfully, no one had been injured. A full description of the lone robber was broadcast over the county radio and sent to neighboring police departments that were not part of the countywide system. The major crime unit of the Morris County Prosecutor's Office was notified along with the Newark branch of the FBI. Investigators and a special agent from the FBI responded to the scene. Because this bank had been located in a strip mall in our town, all the store workers and patrons present at the time of the robbery were questioned, and all the businesses were canvassed for possible witnesses. Another detective from our police department who had not been working that day was called in to assist during the investigation. I was the senior and lead detective on this case.

The bank had opened at 9:00 a.m., and the robbery had occurred at 9:05 a.m. Interviewing all the bank employees made for a long day. The amount of money taken during the robbery had not been determined immediately. During the subsequent days, leads were established and pursued. I arranged to meet with all the other agencies who might have had previous dealings with this bank robber based on his M.O. (modus operandi) and description. Apparently, he had worn the same baseball cap and jacket during seven previous bank robberies he had committed in Morris and Essex Counties. At this task force meeting, we developed more information about a particular suspect. I have to admit that I really enjoyed working a case like this one instead of a noise complaint case.

Then the FBI contacted me to arrange for a task force meeting at their Newark office to discuss the robbery. I attended the meeting as did other detectives from the area. I went into the meeting with the wrong impression regarding its purpose. You see, I had assumed that it was going to be an information-sharing meeting that would facilitate our making an arrest in the case together. I had developed several excellent leads and was going in the right direction. The FBI had nothing to share with us while I, on the other hand, had information packets for all the agencies. I was paired up with an investigator from the Morris County Prosecutor's Office for some of the surveillance work. Surveillance could be very boring, especially when nothing was going on, and you were just watching a house or a vehicle. I decided to bring one of my textbooks with me because I was attending Seton Hall University for my master's degree. My partner and I would take turns, and during my down time, I would read chapters in my textbook. My particular partner at that time was Jim Gannon, who is now Sheriff of Morris County.

Days passed with no new leads. I was on surveillance in Union City when I got called back to the chief's office. When I arrived at headquarters, I was told to break off the surveillance on that particular home and individual. I was bewildered and asked why. Apparently, the FBI was building a bigger case against the individual whom I had been surveilling.

I was a little disappointed, but then I was able to vacation with my family for the last two weeks of August before school started. We vacationed in Vermont that summer, and I called in to headquarters frequently for any news on the bank robbery. The case went inactive for a few months, but later that winter the same individual whom I been surveilling was arrested in Texas. He was charged with a bank robbery there and with all the bank robberies in our area. Case closed!

Animal House

When you've been a police officer for a few years, you know when certain types of calls will occur or, I should say, more of an occurrence of certain types of calls. We could always count on graduation parties to commence in May and end sometime in June after school ended. I remember responding one evening with other officers to a few rather large parties. One of them I recall was on Huron Drive; a few neighbors had called up to report that there were many teens coming and going and the neighbors knew the parents were not home. The responding patrol units had to park a good distance away, and we walked up to the residence. As we approached the residence, we could see what appeared to be teenagers in all the front rooms of the home and even on the second floor. It looked like a scene from Animal House, no wonder the neighbors called. We could also see them holding beer cans and bottles in their hands. As we got closer to the front door, we could see the teens running from room to room, spilling the beer and some scrambling to the basement. We had teens come out on the second floor balcony and jump and run into the woods so they wouldn't be caught. There were only a few officers and at least fifty or more teens. A few of the teens and the homeowner's son were taken into custody and transported to police headquarters. Since they were juveniles, their parents were called and had to respond to headquarters to bring them home. When we asked the hard question, where did the beer come from?, we usually got the standard answer: "I found it" or "a friend gave it to me", and no one knew the friend's name. When the homeowners arrived home, they were not pleased either to find out what had happened or to find their home trashed.

That's no burglar, that's my son!

A few times in my career, I received a call from the dispatcher that a neighbor saw someone climbing through a window of a home. This particular incident occurred in the Wickham Woods section of town. It was a little past midnight when the call was received. A full description was provided by the neighbor. The neighbor himself was out late that evening and was pulling into his driveway and saw a guy climbing through a second story window. Second story burglaries at night are very rare in most communities and especially ours. I responded and checked the residence and saw a ladder up against the back of the house. Another patrol officer was stationed in front of the house. I could see that there were no lights on in the house, and both cars were in the opened garage and cold to the touch.

I rang the bell and had our dispatcher call the residence to come and meet me at the door. The residents did meet me and, after explaining the reason for our visit, allowed me to gain entry to their second floor. They immediately brought me to their teenage son's room, opened the door; and the clothes lying on the floor were the same ones the neighbor reported seeing. After a brief conversation with their son, he admitted to being out too late and had forgotten his key; and didn't want to wake up anyone. We let the parents decide on the course of action with their son.

It's after 10 pm, do you know where your children are?

On one of the many midnight shifts on patrol, I was travelling on Southern Boulevard near the mall by Hickory Tree Garage. It was just around 2 a.m., and I had just finished checking all the businesses in the two malls when a vehicle passed me with its windows all iced up. I turned around and activated my overhead lights, stopped the vehicle, and approached the vehicle. The driver looked too young to have a driver's license and the other occupant did also. My backup arrived and was at the passenger side door. The registration was called into headquarters for ownership. When the ownership of the vehicle came back, it was not the same name, nor could the driver tell me the correct address of where the car was registered. After a few minutes and a few more questions, nothing was adding up with these boys. I had our dispatcher contacted the owner of the vehicle. Once the owner was contacted, he indicated to our dispatcher that the car was brought to the garage to have work done on it. The driver apparently left the keys to the car under the mat in the unlocked car. The boys finally admitted that they had been home, set their alarm for midnight, snuck out of the house, and walked to the garage in hopes of finding an open car -- and they did!

The best part is coming. The boys (juveniles 16 years of age) were arrested and transported to headquarters to be picked up by their parents. One of the boy's parents responded immediately and took custody of him. The other boy, the driver's father, didn't believe that we had his son. He was actually giving our dispatcher a hard time, saying that we had nothing better to do than to wake him up and accuse his son when he knew that his son was asleep in his room. This particular family lived in the Green Village's section of town near Spring Valley Road. I called the father back and said to him, "Humor me, go and check your son's room, I'll wait on the phone". Less than two minutes later the father said, in a much different tone, "I'll be right there."

A few minutes later, the boy's father arrived with a different attitude, thanking us, and was not too happy about his son's actions. I informed the father, as I did with the other set of parents, that our juvenile officer will be in contact and, as a result of this, would probably go to juvenile court. The father said to me, "That won't be necessary, I'll handle it from here, officer". "No, that's not how it works," I told him. The father's attitude changed yet again. "Do you know who I am?" he said. I said, "Yes, I do, and thank you for reminding me". Apparently, he thought being a prominent lawyer with an office in Morristown was going to exempt his son from any consequences. Because his son had prior infractions with the police, he and his accomplices were dealt with in juvenile court in Morristown and placed on probation.

Concluding remarks

I have pulled dead, mangled bodies from cars. I have lied to people as they were dying. I said you were going to be fine as I held their hand and watch life fade from them (too many times). I remember one Christmas week responding to five medical assist calls, and all five of which turned out to be fatal heart attacks or massive strokes. I fought with people who wanted to stab me and shoot me. I was attacked by women who had had the shit kicked out of them by their husbands as I was arresting them. I did CPR when I knew there was no hope, but did it to make the family feel better. I have torn down doors, chased bad guys through the woods, engaged in high-speed chases, and helped deliver babies. I have arrested many people and I have given many breaks (discretion) and prayed for people I did not even know. I used necessary force when I had to and was kind when I could be.

When people were running away from a scene for fear, I was running towards it to help.

There were a few times I drove myself to a secluded place and shed tears over a call. I missed many Christmases and other holidays with my family far more than I wanted to. Every cop I know has done this -- and more.

I am extremely proud of my sons who are police officers and represent four generations of law enforcement officers in our family.

Would I do it again? In a heartbeat!

About the Author

Dr. James F. Ford, Jr. (Jim) currently serves as a Professor of Criminal Justice and Director of the Graduate Program in Justice Administration and Public Service at the College of Saint Elizabeth, in Morristown, New Jersey. Prior to becoming a professor at the College of Saint Elizabeth, Jim was an adjunct at the College, the County College of Morris, and Grand Canyon University, Phoenix, AZ.

Prior to becoming an academic, Jim began his law enforcement career in 1976 with the Chatham Township Police Department in New Jersey. Over his career, he served in the patrol, investigative and administrative divisions. While working patrol, he served as a patrol officer, traffic safety officer, and a crime prevention officer. In 1987, Jim became a member of the detective bureau and was responsible for all criminal investigations. In 1990, Jim was promoted to the rank of Sergeant and assigned to the patrol division, where he was responsible for a platoon of officers. In 1999 Jim was promoted to the rank of Lieutenant. As a Lieutenant, Jim was in charge of the Patrol Division, In-Service Training, Rules and Regulations, Policies and Procedures, Research and Planning, Public Information Officer, and the Office of Emergency Management. Jim retired with the rank of Lieutenant from the Chatham Township Police Department after 26 years of service.

Besides his teaching responsibilities in undergraduate and graduate programs, Jim has served on many academic committees, groups, and clubs at the College of Saint Elizabeth. These include Academic Life, Budgetary Committee, Academic Technology Committee (which he served as Chairperson), Middle States Evaluation Committee, and Criminal Justice Advisory Board. He has also brokered partnership with the International Police Association, Morristown Police Department, and Florham Park Police to name a few. Jim also oversees the hiring of qualified instructors and mentors them in the undergraduate and graduate criminal justice programs.

In 2007, Jim conducted a feasibility study, and conducted extensive research into the College of Saint Elizabeth becoming the first college in New Jersey to offer a fully online master's degree in criminal justice. In the fall of 2009, the program was launched and other colleges and universities followed. The program began with only six students and today has over thirty-five. The program was also ranked #3 Nationwide by Affordable Colleges Online.

U.S. News and World Reports currently ranks our M.A. program in Justice Administration and Public Service in the top 25!

Jim presented a Poster Board exhibit and was a panel member at the Work Life Symposium National Conference in Washington, DC, on the hazards of shift work. He also published criminal justice articles with the International Police Association Region #10 Newsletter, NJ Cops, and NJ Blue Now magazines.

Jim published his first book which is available on Amazon titled, *Shift Work and Criminal Justice Professionals.*

Jim earned his bachelor's degree from Glassboro State College (Rowan University), his master's degree from Seton Hall University, and his doctorate from Capella University in Minneapolis, MN. He is a certified New Jersey Police Training Instructor and a graduate of CPM (Certified Public Manager Program) through Rutgers University and the State of New Jersey Personnel Department.

Additionally, Jim remains an active member of many organizations: New Jersey State Police Benevolent Association (Life Time-Gold Member), New Jersey State Crime Prevention Officers Association, New Jersey State Traffic Officers Association, Chatham Township PBA #170, Gold Life Member and former PBA Delegate, New Jersey Association of Criminal Justice Educators, Academy of Criminal Justice Sciences, New Jersey Licensed Private Investigators and the International Police Officers Association, and Advocate for New Jersey Veterans Network.

Jim resides in Union, New Jersey, with his wife Debbie. He is the proud father of three grown married children: Brian, Kelly, and Timothy, and he is a grandfather to Juliana,

Charlie, Matteo, Sam, and Cayleigh. Jim and his wife also own a residence in Bethel, Vermont where they love to fish, snowmobile, and enjoy the country life.

CPSIA information can be obtained
at www.ICGtesting.com
Printed in the USA
FFOW02n0023090218
44948285-45220FF